The Hand
of God

The Hand of God

of God

Tony Acree

Hydra Publications
1310 Meadowridge Trail
Goshen, Kentucky 40026

ISBN:0615913644

Printed in the United States of America

www.hydrapublications.com

For my family: my wife Karin, daughters Katy and Lauren, and my mom and dad. They keep the magic alive.

Chapter One

It was 6 P.M. when the Devil walked into my office and had a seat.

Now when I say the Devil, I'm not talking figuratively. Lord knows that having spent the last five years as a bounty hunter, I've come face to face with every form of evil that walks on this scum-ridden planet: murderers, rapists, even a couple of freakin' child molesters. So I have more than a passing acquaintance with evil, of both the male and female varieties.

But no, in this case, I'm talking in the literal sense. You know, as in Satan, Lucifer, Beelzebub, the goddamned Father of all goddamned Lies. That Devil.

You're probably wondering if he was all red, with horns, a pointed tail and pitchfork. Sorry to disappoint you, but he wasn't. He looked like any other well-dressed bastard in a snazzy suit and shoes to match. OK, he did have a red tie, but I couldn't see any tail coming out his ass. He was around six feet tall, blond hair and icy blue eyes. Guess we know where Hitler got his ideas for all that superior race crap.

And I bet you're also wondering just how the hell I knew it was the Fallen Angel himself. I guess it was the same way Moses knew that the burning bush was really God and not just a couple of his buddies lighting the damned thing on fire and then pretending to be God while hiding behind the closest rock laughing. Let's put it this way, if the Devil walks through your door one day, you won't have any doubts either. Take my word for it.

Anyway, I'd had a good week and was just getting ready to leave and lock the place up, looking forward to taking the weekend off from chasing bad guys and heading down to Molly Malone's, when the door opened and in waltzed Satan, just as pretty as you please. He pulled up a chair near my desk and sat down flashing a row of pearly whites the Kardashian family would be proud of.

"Victor, you know who I am?" he said, eyebrows all arched and superior, although it was more of a proclamation than a question.

I nodded back and calmly opened the top right drawer of my desk and grabbed my Glock 9 millimeter I keep there in case of emergencies. I figured if this didn't qualify for an emergency then nothing would.

"You know that won't do you any good," he said.

He was right. Somehow I knew that. After all, for more than a couple of millennium at a bare minimum, people have wanted to kick Satan's backside with no success. I just knew it wouldn't do me any good.

But I pulled the gun out and shot the son-of-a-bitch right between the eyes anyway. Blamo!

A perfect gun powdered entry wound appeared smack dab between his eyes. But I could see no blood and no head explosion out the back, just a big hole and an annoyed look on Satan's formerly pristine mug.

Now you would think that a guy, after being shot in the head, would exhibit some sort of adverse effects, but not this time. And folks, that's just wrong.

I asked myself, "Why did I do that?" and the only thing I could come up with was that I was trying to score some brownie points with the big guy upstairs, you know, just in case I ever made it to the Heavenly gates.

Guess I should mention that's something else that happened right when he walked in. I became a full-fledged believer in God right there on the spot. I mean, if the Devil exists, you can bet to holy high heaven that God does, too.

Funny thing was, before then? I wasn't what one would call an overly "religious" person. To be honest, I never gave it much thought as to whether God existed or not. Life was what it was and no God was going to change that. So why should I worry about it? I think the only time I ever did talk about God was at the end of the night with my buddies down at the bar and I was usually dead ass drunk.

But right then and there I became what I guess you would call, born again. I immediately promised God that I would be a three times a week church going, down on my knees praying, holier than thou living son of a gun if I could just keep on breathing awhile longer. Amen.

And you know there was another thing that happened that I was surprised about, too. I wasn't out of my boots afraid and pissing my pants right there in my chair. After all, they don't come any more frightening than old Lucifer, right? But instead of being afraid? I felt edgy, and more alive. And I knew what he wanted.

"You can't have it," I said.

"I don't want it," he shot back.

"Huh?" And here people say I'm not a great conversationalist.

"I don't want your soul," he replied. His accent sounded like he'd lived here in Louisville all his life. I thought he was going to have a deep otherworldly kind of voice, or at least a British-sounding accent like in all those horror flicks where people get possessed and then commit all kinds of stupid evil acts. Seems the Devil always has a British accent.

"I'm confused," I said, and I'm sure it showed all over my face. "I just figured--"

"That's the problem with your feeble-minded people," he said smoothing out his lapel, still with that nasty bullet hole in his head, bugging me more now than it was obviously bothering him. "Always trying to figure things out. Idiots, really. But, if you're giving your soul away, sure, I'll take it. What I want, though, is to hire you. I want you to find someone for me."

Well, I couldn't help but feel a tad uncomfortable. I figured if the Devil needed help and he was looking at me, I was in a bit of a bind. "If that's all you want, the answer is No. Not even if hell itself freezes over. By the way, has that ever happened?" I couldn't help but be curious.

He ignored the question and continued, "Oh, you'll take the job," he said with a confidence that made the hair stand up all over my freakin' body. It pissed me off.

"You can keep your 30 pieces of silver or whatever in hell else you plan on offering me," I said, "I won't do it."

Then he pulled out a sheet of paper from his inner suit pocket. "This," he said holding the paper out so I could see it, "Is a soul contract."

"You've got to be kidding me," I said. I always thought that was just some more movie made up bullshit, like in that bad Brendan Frazier movie. "But you've already mentioned you don't want my soul. So I guess lying is something that comes natural for someone in your line of work?"

"This isn't for you, my friend," he said. I didn't like that he was calling me 'friend.' "This one has already been signed: by your big brother, of all people."

Now, when my mom introduces Michael Christopher McCain as my big brother, people have a tendency to snicker. I'm six and a half feet tall and nearly three-hundred pounds and 'big bro' has to work hard to reach five foot nothing and one-hundred and forty pounds soaking wet. The only thing that makes him bigger is that he's six years older than me and is a bigger prick.

My yahoo of a brother spends most of his life trying to overcompensate for his shortcomings, with one over-the-top scheme after another. After high school, hell, you name it, he tried it: selling Amway, timeshares, cars, and even opening up his own line of car washes, but the sucker investors took the bath, not the damned cars.

Yes, sir. Vic McCain's older brother struck out more times than a blind one-armed batter hitting in a hurricane. But that all seemed to change about five years ago.

He opened this import-export business. I asked how he was planning on exporting the manure I was sure he was spreading around. Next thing you know? His warehouses are full of stuff and he's moving goods around the world—and making money hand over fist.

He went from driving a beat up old Honda to a brand spanking new Lexus 400 convertible. He even loaned me the cash to get my bounty hunting business up and running. With interest, of course.

But now, with the Devil sitting in front of me dangling this piece of paper, I knew just how Mikey boy had broken the ole' piggy bank. Step right up: One soul for sale. Attention Wal-Mart shoppers. And Satan closed the deal and was more than willing to make another purchase.

I never thought a smile could be so…evil looking. The Devil's eyes lit up like the sparkles the sun makes when it hits ripples on a mountain lake. It was in stark contrast to that bull's-eye blackened hole I tattooed on his forehead.

He spoke. "You see, in twenty-four hours your brother will die. It will be horrible, and he will suffer. Badly. I'm honestly looking forward to it. It will be bloody. There will be screaming. He'll sound like a little girl in the end, pleading for his soul."

"Oh, and I want you to know how this works," he said leaning a bit forward. "One of the conditions of his contract is that his heart must still be beating when I claim my possession. He must be aware I have taken his everlasting soul." He leaned back into the chair comfortably and continued. "I think it's more fun for me that way, really. Seeing the realization that a man has abandoned his God for a pittance of earthly glory. It just makes me… giddy."

"But let me be perfectly clear, the writhing pain and torment he will be experiencing when I rip his heart from his chest will be minuscule compared to what the rest of eternity will hold for him." He leaned forward and gave me a barracuda grin. "Let me give you just a taste of what lies ahead for your brother."

And he snapped his fingers.

In an instant, I was nailed to a wall by my hands, shoulders, stomach, knees, and feet by large barbed spikes. My arms were above my head and my legs were spread eagle to near the breaking point. Flames were dancing all over my body and I could smell the sour odor of my flesh as it burned away to expose the muscle and bone underneath. Worst of all, there was a mirror on the wall across from me and I was watching it all happen. I couldn't look away, no matter how hard I tried. My whole body just started to melt and slide downward, like a wax museum statue tossed on this year's Halloween bonfire. And I could see it all and I howled as my nervous system sent the pain from the heat crashing into my brain. My lungs were scorched as I breathed in the flames and I wished I would die. But I didn't.

The next instant I was standing up back in my office. Sweat flowed out from every pore of my body and my heart thundered inside my ears. My stomach tried hard to reverse engines with today's lunch, but I resisted. The smell of sulfur still clogged my nose and lungs as my breath was coming in great 'Please, Lord, let the air back in my body' wheezes. I fought, but finally lost the battle as I vomited into a garbage can next to my desk. I rubbed my arms as the pain lingered from my flesh being set on fire. I couldn't blink from the shock I just experienced. It may have only been seconds? It felt like forever.

The Devil looked casually down at his hands and thumbed over his well-manicured nails. "Anyway," he said, "That's what will happen, over and over for eternity, to your only brother unless you do exactly what I say."

I'm not overly close to my brother, honestly. But dear God, I can't let this happen to him. I can't.

I dropped down in my big swivel chair because, quite frankly, my legs were going all jelly doughnuts on me. I tried to get my mind around what was going on, but something didn't make any sense.

I said, "Why me? Why can't you find this guy? Hell, why can't you find anyone on God's green earth any time you want?"

"It's not *God's* green earth," he snarled, anger flashing through those ice blue eyes, "It's mine. He may hold sway in Heaven…for the moment. But not here." My eyes opened up a bit and my breathing stopped, but then he took a moment and regained his composure, so I did, too.

"Besides," he said, "It's not a man that I need: it's a woman. And finding her is not something I can just 'do'. Not even the so-called Almighty can just tap the shoulder of anyone He needs. People, with their damned free will, have to be found. And I don't want to waste my time. You mortals and your vanity in thinking that He and I both keep track of your every waking moment disgusts me."

I couldn't help myself after that comment, so I said, "If anyone would know about vanity, I'm betting that would be you. After all, isn't that what got your sorry butt kicked to the basement to begin with? Thinking you were better than God? From what I've heard, you got yours handed to you in a sling." I was beginning to recover from my near hell experience and I would be damned, so to speak, if I was going to let him lecture me about good and evil. I mean, come on.

He stood slowly and reached inside his jacket. I tensed, ready for just about anything. I didn't know if he was going to strike me down with a bolt of lightning or throw sickness dust on me to make me suffer. All he did, though, was pull out another sheet of paper and drop it on the desk. I wondered how this paper was going to kill me.

He said, "This is who I want, her name and last known address. Bring her to me, here, in twenty-four hours. If you do as I ask, I will tear up your brother's contract and his immortal soul will be returned to him. If you don't? Your brother will die and his soul will forever burn in hell."

"Why?" I said. "What do you want this woman for?"

"The reasons are my own. Just have her by six tomorrow evening." Opening the door, he turned back. "Make sure she's alive, Victor. If she comes to me otherwise…"

He let the thought trail off. "I get the picture, butt-head."

The Devil looked at me and flashed those politician teeth. "I like your spirit, Vic," he said, and then he laughed, just like he always does in the movies, as he strolled out the door.

Chapter Two

For a moment, I just sat there, my mind numb with the implications of taking on a job for Satan. And more importantly, I thought about what it meant for my brother if I didn't.

I snatched up the phone and dialed my brother's cell. I just knew he was going to answer and I'd find out I was having one hell of a bad daydream brought on by a stressful job and way too many quarter pounders with cheese.

But when Mikey Boy answered the phone, it became clear all this was way too real.

"Oh Jesus Christ, Vic, I'm screwed!" he yelled into the phone. He sounded out of breath and as if he was running like his life depended on it. Bingo, Mikey Boy.

"Mikey, where are you? What's happening?"

Mikey let out a scream. It sounded like he fell, his cell phone bouncing across the ground. There was a moment of silence that had me gritting my teeth, picturing all manner of very bad things that could be happening to him when Satan picked up my bro's phone and said, "You're wasting time, Victor. Don't you have better things to do right now?"

The line went dead. I just hope my brother didn't go dead with it. I slammed the receiver back down in frustration.

There had to be a way out of this, though for the life of me, I couldn't see what it was. All I could do, for now, was find the girl. That, at least, would give me some options. If I could find out why Satan wanted her, I might find the leverage I could use to free my brother and not hand over the girl. Helping Satan had to be bad for the world in general, the girl in particular. Somehow I had the feeling this wasn't going to be a stroll through the park.

Ninety percent of all bail jumpers are caught by bounty hunters, not cops, as we have advantages the cops don't. In most states, I don't need a warrant to bust your door down and drag your sorry ass to jail. I don't need an extradition hearing to take you across state lines. I just need the trunk of my car. When a felon signs on with a bail bondsman, he signs away any rights he might otherwise have expected.

But what the cops and I both need, in most cases, is time. It can take weeks, even months to catch some wayward criminal. I had twenty-four hours. And just what would be the chances of me catching her sitting at home, watching Oprah, just waiting for the bounty hunter of her dreams, to come waltzing through her door to whisk her away to a future life with the king of all evil, Satan? About as much chance as I have of getting a date with Sandra Bullock: El-Zippo, her mistake with Jessie James notwithstanding.

The information on the girl was typed on standard computer paper in regular black ink. The fact it wasn't done in blood was somehow disappointing.

The note was short and to the point: Miranda Olivia Chernenko, 540 South Third Street, Apartment 2A. That was it, a name and address. Thanks a whole heap there Satan, ole' buddy.

I fired up my computer and started a skip trace on Ms. Miranda. As I did, my mind wandered down a path foreign to any previous thinking I'd ever done. I mean, Christ, the Devil doesn't just sashay on in and tell you he needs you to do work for him…not unless there was something biblical associated with the request.

Biblical. Listen to me. I was thinking Molly Malone's for dinner not more than 30 minutes ago. Now the word biblical was consuming my thoughts. I laughed at myself for that one. Biblical. Bible. God. What did I know of God? As far as I knew, life was just a frickin' biological journey of birth, growth, and death, with a little sex in the middle there to pass the time and give a person a sense of belonging. If you were lucky, lots of sex. If you were really, really lucky, you died while having sex.

But now, it was different. Heaven was in the picture. Heaven…God…Jesus, what have I gotten myself into? Before the Devil showed up, life eternal meant nothing to me. Now, life eternal was looming over me like the executioner's ax.

I'd never really pictured myself as the strumming harps kind of guy. I wanted to live, and then die. Go out with the knowledge that that was it. That I'd done everything I could do. Now it was over. But Nooooooo. Now, there were the harps, pearly gates, sitting on clouds, strumming endlessly. I wondered if there was sex in heaven. I wondered a lot of things.

I snapped out of it as the computer beeped letting me know it was ready. I ran Miranda Olivia Chernenko through all the major databases: criminal check, social security, motor vehicle, Nexus-Lexus, etc. Nothing. Go figure. I Googled her and came up bupkis. As far as cyberspace was concerned, she didn't exist. And if you don't exist there, what type of life are you leading, anyways?

The street address, 540 South Third St. Apt. 2A, was down in Old Louisville, near the University of Louisville. I decided that trying to dig up anything else on her here was wasting time. Devil or no, my brother was in trouble and it looked like I was the only one in the world who could help. I grabbed my gun and my keys and walked over to the door the Devil had walked through a short time before.

I paused. If I turned the knob and walked through the door, would there be Hell or a hallway on the other side? Seemed to me there was a better than average chance I just died from a heart attack, with the Devil playing a cruel joke. He could be there in Hell laughing at me right now, which, I suppose, he was doing regardless.

Walking through the door would be like walking through the portal to the rest of my sorry existence. I decided, actually very quickly, it didn't make one goddamned bit of difference one way or the other. I've never been much on second guessing or worrying about things I'd no control over.

I grabbed the knob, turned it, and walked out into the hallway of the same building in which I'd been working for the last several years. No flames, no flickering shadows, no evilness... just the hard wood floors and taupe wall paint. "If this is Hell, it's bland," I said to myself as I flipped the light off in the hallway and walked out into the damp early evening air.

Chapter Three

Sitting in my car, waiting at the light in front of the Burger King, I looked at the address on the Devil's typed piece of paper. The only option available to me meant heading to her place. If she wasn't just sitting around waiting for the Devil to find her, I would toss the place and see what I could dig up. I mean, after all, how much trouble could I get myself into? I had the frickin' Devil as a client. What? Did I think the Louisville police force would be a big deal if they showed up? "I'm so sorry, officer, about the breaking and entering. But, I'm going to Hell soon. So I thought, why not?"

I shook my head, the light turned green. I turned and floored up the entrance ramp onto I-64. I made the fifteen miles to Spaghetti Junction in twelve minutes. Now there's a piece of highway that Satan must have had a hand in developing. I slowed a bit to make the off ramp onto I-65, but the tires of my red '69 Chevelle squealed constantly around the turn anyway. Two exits later I made my way into the part of town known as Old Louisville. Here the houses are beautifully maintained Victorian mansions from the late 1800s. The yards are small and usually bordered by black wrought iron fences with little spearheads on each one. Dickens would have fit right at home.

Today, many of these old brick homes are sectioned into duplexes or quad apartments for University students to inhabit. This was the case for number 540. I parked on the street staying just out of the glow of one of the many street lamps and locked my gun in the glove box. If I got busted while in the apartment, no use adding armed robbery to the charge. I walked up the 5 concrete steps to the large covered porch.

The white columns supporting the roof were adorned with hanging baskets of bleeding hearts and ivy, and the oval leaded glass on the front door seemed to sag in its black painted heavy wood frame. I turned the slightly tarnished brass knob and walked into the lighted foyer. So much for security.

There was a door on each side of the main entryway on the first level, 1A and 1B. There was a single antique glass lamp hanging from a decorative chain in the center of the twelve-foot ceiling. It illuminated the curved wooden banister and wooden steps going up, and then turned to continue on to the second floor. I looked at the paper again. 2A. I went up.

The upper foyer was identical to the lower, except it had a large double hung window with stained glass in the place of the front door and a soft single bulb light overhead. There were two apartments. I rapped softly on apartment 2A's door. I didn't expect anything, but wanted to alleviate any suspicions from the residents of 2B in case they heard my arrival.

When no one came to the door, I reached into my jacket pocket, pulled out my trusty set of lock picks, and made short work of the skeleton-keyed bolt. I was lucky. You always see guys busting these locks on TV in less time than it takes to get a beer from the fridge during a commercial, but they can be a pain in the ass sometimes.

I quickly and quietly opened the door half-way, and slid in. I shut it behind me, holding the knob in my hand so as not to make a click with the latch. Then I let the knob loose slowly, relocked the door, flipped a light switch on, and turned to look at the apartment.

Her place was very nice and not typical of the starving college students that cycled through this area every four years. Ethan Allen furniture filled the room, arranged in a manner that would make the finest of those wacko cable show interior decorators envious. A large brick fireplace crouched on the far wall, with an Oriental rug under the coffee table. Bistro lights over the breakfast bar marked the physical border between the gourmet kitchen and living room. The place smelled of fine leather. The place screamed money. One large window, the blinds partially drawn, looked out over a small side yard between this house and the next. But no girl.

I shut the blinds the rest of the way and went straight to the bedroom. Here it became clear this was a chick's place. No bachelor's pad in history was this neat. Her bedroom had the same quality of furniture I'd found in the living room: four poster bed, matching dresser and armoire. A computer desk was placed along one wall, a brand spanking new Dell (complete with twenty-one inch flat screen) parked on top. The annoying little Windows icon bounced around the PC gleefully in obvious screen saver mode. I stuck my head into the bathroom, just to make sure she wasn't hiding out in the shower. But again, no luck. I stood for a moment, looking around. Odd. I found no pictures or wall hangings anywhere in the room. I glanced back out into the main room. Same thing. Nada. Since when did any babe not have 'things' hanging on the walls? There were no pictures anywhere in the apartment. So, I still didn't have a clue what Ms. Chernenko looked like.

I tossed the room, emptying every dresser drawer, her armoire, and the one small closet. I didn't bother being neat about it, just throwing the stuff on the floor. I didn't have nearly enough time to be Mr. Clean. If I found her, I'd apologize. When I finished, I still found nothing giving me the least little bit of info on my mark, other than she dresses well, uses Channel No. 5 perfume, and is a neat freak. Won't she be happy when she gets home?

I moved to the PC, taking a seat in the small swivel chair, my ass feeling like it was going to sink right through it any moment. I moved the mouse and her desktop came to life. I just thanked God she didn't password protect her stuff. People will never learn.

I clicked on the icon and jumped straight to her email. This chick needed a spam filter in the worst sort of way. One email did jump out from the rest of the garbage littering her Inbox. It was dated today at 1 P.M., from someone using the name TheDevilMadeMeDoIt, with a subject title of *8 P.M. Tonight*. Bingo.

I double-clicked the email and the rest of it appeared. It read:.

I am willing to meet you. Tonight, 8 P.M., at The Down and Dirty Bar on Bardstown Road. How will I recognize you? This will be the only time I am willing to do this. If you are not there, don't contact me again.

That was it, short and sweet. No signed name. I closed the email and clicked on her Sent items. She sent a response at 1:06 P.M. indicating she would be there with her hair tied back in a red scarf and wait at the bar, so that he would know who she was.

I checked her machine for any other information. Her My Documents and My Pictures folder was as empty as a Hobo's soup pan. This woman truly had no life.

Something started to bother me. I glanced around the bedroom. Everything was showroom new, with not a nick, scratch, or dent of any kind. Even the PC was new.

I walked back out to the living room. All brand-spanking new. You could have been standing on a showroom floor, with the only thing missing being the price tags. Even the garbage can in the kitchen was empty. Something just didn't feel right.

It was then that my train of thought was derailed by a sound coming from the front door. Holy crap: someone was trying to pick the lock!

I flipped off the lights, plunging the room into near darkness. I took pleasure as whoever it was picking the lock took much longer than I did to break in. Finally, the lock made a soft click, followed by a moment of silence. I rested a finger on the door and could feel someone slowly turn the knob and open it.

I couldn't help but think this girl was turning out to be way too popular. I positioned myself behind the door. As it opened I knew immediately I was in trouble.

The hallway light no longer offered up its reassuring glow outside the door, having either been unscrewed or busted out, which left little doubt as to the intentions of the new folks.

My eyes, now adjusted to the darkness, allowed me to see three fairly large individuals move into the room. I had no doubt how I would handle this situation. They were in the apartment illegally, clearly up to no good. The mere fact I'd done exactly the same thing was beside the point. These guys were interfering with my objectives and that meant I needed to find out what they were doing here and why. If I'd brought my gun with me this would already be over, but I hadn't.

I got the feeling that just asking, "Hey fellas, just what the Sam hell you think you're doing?" wasn't going to work. Physicality was needed. When I was young, my father taught me that the person who fought fair when he was out numbered or when his or her life was on the line, was the chump that was going to get their ever lovin' ass kicked. Fighting by Marquis de Queensberry rules is for idealistic dreamers with good medical insurance.

I took one large step to the left, putting me right behind the three intruders. When fighting more than one guy there are several things to consider. Surprise is number one and I had it. They should have looked behind the door, but the dumb asses didn't. So they were sure as Hell going to be surprised when I lowered the boom on them. Second, you don't want a long-term fight. Hit them hard, fast and continuously and put as many of them on the ground as quickly as possible. Don't hold back. And lastly, you need to stay off the ground yourself. Once you go down, when outnumbered, you're staying down. So you need to choose a plan putting them on the ground while you remain King of the Mountain.

There may be no quicker way of taking a guy down from behind, short of using lethal force, than a kidney punch. The pain is intense, like being kicked in the balls. Hit them hard enough and the person is guaranteed to collapse and may fall into shock. It's possible to even kill someone with a kidney punch. Boxing outlaws the punch for a reason.

I hit the guy directly in front of me, rotated at the hips and shot my right arm out from my waist with enough force to take out a baby bull, hitting him in his lower back, on the right. He collapsed, screaming in pain, and dropped something to the ground he was holding in his hands. I shoved him into the guy on the left, taking them to the ground. As they fell, I saw a flash and heard a hiss as Taser darts flew by my head, hitting into the wall behind me.

Jesus, I hate those things. There are as much as fifty-thousand volts in one shot and just the thought of that much Ben Franklin juice coursing through my veins made me shiver. And it made me hesitate a fraction of a second, giving the one guy left standing his chance and he took it, connecting with a left cross to my jaw. I turned with the punch, reducing the blow, but it still stung like a nest of hornets had landed on my cheek. It staggered me back a step and I tripped over the other two guys, crashing down on top of Miss Chernenko's new coffee table, splintering it into firewood. So much for no scratches or dents in the furniture.

I rolled over and kicked out hard with both legs just as he bore down on top of me. He reversed directions, flying hard up and over the love seat, taking out a lamp for good measure.

I started to get to my feet. The guy I kidney punched was still down, while the other guy frantically searched for the missing item on the floor. He saw me rising and dove into me, taking me back off my feet, and believe me, that's no easy trick.

We thrashed about on the floor and he ended up on top of me, smelling of too much garlic and more than a touch of Kentucky bourbon. I shifted my weight, preparing to flip him, when I felt cold steel pressing against my throat.

"Brother, make one more move and I'll slice you cleaner than a

Thanksgiving turkey." He remained on top of me, with only my right arm free, but I let my body relax. One, because he had a knife to my throat. Second, because even though I couldn't see his face, I knew who it was. That voice was all J.B.

James Allan Booker, J.B. to his friends and associates, is the second best bounty hunter in the area, right behind me, of course. A black man in his middle forties, J.B. has been around the block a few times. Growing up in the projects in Louisville's West End, his youth was spent dodging gangs, the law, and whoever else might want a piece of his hide.

Tough neighborhoods and tough situations were nothing to J.B. He was a survivor. After doing a stint as an MP in Uncle Sam's Army, he moved back to Louisville. Looking for work, a bondsman gave him a job hunting down jumpers. He was good at it and found out he liked it.

If there was a knock on J.B.'s resume, it was that his returned jumpers came back a little more banged up than most others. But who was going to complain about a bail skipper getting a few more bruises on the return trip.

"J.B., is that you, ole' buddy ole' pal?" I said in my most friendly how the hell are ya kind of tone.

"Well I'll be damned, Victor McCain." I could hear the surprise in his voice. "You really shouldn't have jumped me and my boys like that."

"My mistake, J.B. Let me buy you a beer and make it up to you."

"Uh-uh, Vic. You ain't movin' till you tell me just what you're doin' here. You must be after the same bitch we are, ain't you? Don't lie to me now."

The warning in his voice wasn't lost on me as his knife continued to press down on my neck, just this side of drawing blood. "Look, J.B., it's important I find the girl. I don't want any trouble with you and yours. Let's just chalk this up to stupid ass fate and let bygones be bygones. You find her first, I'll be there to shake your hand and call you the better bounty hunter. If I find her first…"

"Sorry Vic. Man offered me a lot of green to bring this piece of ass to him straight away. No ways I'm going to give you a chance to mess that up." He paused, and then continued, "I tell you what. Make you a deal. You work for me on this one and I'll split the money with ya. Say, seventy-five twenty-five."

Christ, guess this wasn't going to go well after all. "Let me ask you something, J.B. If our positions were reversed, would you agree to a deal like that? And why shouldn't it be fifty-fifty?" I was stalling, grasping at anything to keep him talking.

Laughing, he said, "Guess not. And no fifty-fifty. I have men to pay and mouths to feed. So if you don't take the offer, too bad. Tell me Vic, I'm guessing the blonde prick that hired me set you after the woman, too. But he wouldn't tell me what the bitch had done to piss him off. You have any ideas?"

All very civil with a knife to my throat. While I didn't think J.B. would slit my throat under normal circumstances, this situation was far from normal. Had Satan offered him a deal like mine? Or was it just pure unadulterated greed that had J.B. a quick motion away from sending me to the other side. Either way, I couldn't afford to wait and see how he would handle the situation.

I could hear the other two guys starting to stir, so time was up. "J.B., the Devil only knows why. But I need you to put your knife down and let me up. Can you do that for me?"

"Sorry, Vic. The Man offered me a ton of cash and I can't pass that up. I just have to figure out what to do with you until that happens. I don't want to cause you any permanent harm, but if you get in my way on this one, someone's going to get hurt and it sure as hell won't be me."

I said, "Thought you were going to say something like that. So let me apologize in advance. I hope you're still able to have a few more kids when this is over."

Unfortunately for J.B., my free hand now held what he'd been searching for: the other guy's Taser. Finding it lying just underneath the couch, I pressed it to J.B.'s crotch. Not hesitating, I pulled the trigger, his balls taking fifty-thousand volts straight up. His body began to spasm and I hurled myself up, throwing him off, with the knife dragging across my skin and drawing blood, but doing no real damage. As for J.B., I don't think he was going to feel much like doing the horizontal bop any time soon.

One of the other guys was just getting to his feet, but I beat him to it. I bull-rushed him, crushing him into the wall, and then dashed out the door. I went down the stairs, stumbling as much as walking, and rubbed my sore jaw where the guy had popped me. Nothing like getting the night off to a great start.

Chapter Four

The clock on the dash flashed 7:34 as I floored the Chevelle, pissed as all get out. I mean, it's bad enough my brother sells his soul to the Devil and I have to bail him out. Add the fact the only hope I have of finding his key to salvation is a woman I don't know, have no description of, and that my only chance of finding her is if she shows up at the Down and Dirty, and if she wears a red scarf and if, if, if.

But for Satan to also sick Booker and his gang onto this woman really ticked me off. I have to work in the same community as these guys. And let's face it, you Taser a guy in the nuts and he isn't likely to keep you on his frickin' Christmas card list. No sir, J.B. was going to want a piece of me and sooner rather than later. Count on it. Nothing like complications.

And why would Satan do that? Besides just being a mean son of a bitch. Did he think I couldn't get the job done? Was he hoping Booker would beat me to the girl and he could then keep my brother's soul as well? Hell, for all I know he was hoping the Beatles would get back together, John and George being dead notwithstanding.

All and all, I guess it really didn't matter much. I still had to find her and try and help my brother. And that's what really pissed me off more than anything. After tossing her place, I knew little more about her now than I did when I started.

I thought about the person she planned to meet, with an email name like Devil Made Me Do It sure sounded like Satan's kind of guy. I wondered if she was planning to sell her soul and this guy was some kind of soul wholesaler? Christ, this sucked.

By my watch, I would be at the Double D in fifteen minutes, and J.B. no more than 30 minutes behind me, at best, if he found the same email—probably less with his extra help and driving like a bat out of hell to catch me. I could only hope that Ms. Chernenko would be there early.

A short time later, I pulled into the parking lot. The place was just a square concrete slab, one story building. No lights illuminated either the parking lot or the building itself, with the exception of the purple neon sign mounted above the door proclaiming the name of the place, though both D's bounced between flickering and out. Who the hell thinks of these dumb-ass bar names, anyway?

Only three cars were parked in the lot: a '72 Monte Carlo with what looked like a gajillion miles on it, a late model Ford Taurus, and a black 2011 Mercedes SLS AMG. The Mercedes stood out like a pimple on a Victoria's Secret super model's face.

I parked the Chevelle next to the Mercedes and got out. I lit a cigarette and took a long drag. People keep telling me that one day they're going to kill me and I've thought about quitting. But tonight, it really didn't seem like black lung disease would be what I would die from. Not the way this day was going. I walked slowly to the door with the cigarette anchored in the corner of my mouth, pushed it open and stepped inside your standard bar.

Round wooden tables filled the center of a large single-room with booths slung along one side of the place. A casual glance told me only four people were there. A man and woman occupied one booth, and they didn't seem to give a rat's patootie about my entrance as they were deep in conversation.

The man was skinny, on the verge of emaciated, and wore a brown mesh baseball cap with a picture of a wrecking truck on the front advertising 'Mike's Towing.' The woman had ratty mid-length hair, no figure to speak of, and nearly as skinny as the man. Both were smoking Marlboro's as fast as they could get them lit, if the overflowing ashtray between them was any clue. Maybe they weren't aware of the city's no smoking ordinance. They were a striking couple and I guessed 'Monte Carlo and Taurus' as I dropped my cig to the floor, grinding it out with the heel of my boot.

There was a jukebox glowing in the corner with its yellow and purple neon bubble trim fighting to be seen through the smoke filled air. Motley Crue was playing, not loud enough to be annoying, but annoying anyway. Next to that, on the far wall, were two shut doors side-by-side with small black signs on them. One of the signs said "Men", the other "omen." There was a gap in the bar next to the 'omen's' room where the bartender could get through, and an opening in the wall beyond leading to a dimly lit back room.

Between the alcohol and the inside edge of the bar, standing there partially turned to the door and to the small portable TV that was mounted in front of the mirror amidst the bottle bleachers, was the bartender. A heavy set, unshaven man, his hairy arms protruded like limbs of a tree from the black t-shirt covering his barrel-chested body. I could just make out a faded Marine Corps tattoo on his left bicep, half-hidden by his shirt. The man bobbed and weaved slightly, sliding his head left then right, his fists clenching and then elevating slightly, while watching a boxing match on the TV.

On the outside edge of the bar, unevenly spaced along its length, were wooden low-back bar stools, all empty, save one. She sat facing the mirror but looking down, a long finger tracing the lip of an empty shot glass. Dressed for a night on the town in a black, mid-thigh evening dress, she slid a glance my way as I approached the bar, then went back to her shot glass. My eyes were drawn to legs any professional dancer would kill for. A red scarf held long blond hair pulled back into a ponytail. Bingo.

They say the path to Hell is paved with good intentions. I had to wonder if I was taking the first of my steps down that path. And then it hit me. I had no earthly idea what I should do next. With a regular perp that I have a legit reason for going after, I would just walk over, handcuff 'em, and drag their sorry ass out. But I didn't have that authority this time. If I forcefully carried her out of here it would be kidnapping. And while the Marlboro twins might not give me any trouble, the guy tending bar looked more than capable of slowing me down until the cops got here, if he got lucky.

I needed to try and come up with a reason to get her out of the bar and fast. J.B. would be here soon. So I needed something that would motivate the lovely Miranda on to her feet and out the door. What I needed was a good pick up line.

I thought of some of the bad pick up lines my brother used when we go bar hopping. Things like, "Excuse me. Do you want to screw or should I just apologize?" Or, "Hey baby, wanna go halves on a bastard?" Good old Mikey boy. He isn't a loser for nothing. I could always go literal and say, "Hey darlin', come with me tonight and I'll show you a Devil of a good time." To hell with it, winging it's always better anyway.

I'm a good enough looking guy. My last girlfriend said I look a little like Chris Hemsworth, the guy who played Thor in the recent comic book movie. Wearing my beat up Wrangler jeans, black T-shirt with the

Bad Samaritan on the front, bomber jacket and boots, I think I'm better looking than he is, but he's richer and has the babes. Guess it's a wash.

Walking to the bar, I slid onto the barstool next to her, got the barkeeps attention and ordered a Miller. On the bar in front of her was a thin black case with gold hinges on the back and matching gold clasps on the front. It was about the size of a pool stick case, but a little longer. This was a bit confusing, since I didn't see any pool tables in this joint. And from her email, I couldn't for the life of me guess why she would be packing around her own stick.

I glanced into the mirror and our eyes met. Green eyes looked back into my baby blues. Mr. Happy started a full salute and I spent a moment trying to get my woody to understand this wasn't going to be his night.

I turned towards her and before I could say anything she said, "I'm not interested."

"I'm sorry, what was that?"

"I'm not interested," she said again.

"Interested in what?"

Her brow furrowed and she said, "In, well, you know."

"No," I said, pausing. "I don't."

She didn't have an accent I could place. Sounded like she might be from the east coast, but it wasn't thick. Her voice was on the soft side and just this side of a purr, carrying an almost sexual quality. This I knew was Mr. Happy's wishful thinking.

The bartender sat the beer in front of me and pointed to her glass. She shook her head No. He gave me a sympathetic look, and then went back to the TV and his boxing match.

She said, "Never mind."

"Oh. You thought I wanted to pick you up, take you back to my place and spend the rest of the night in bed. Sorry, I'd love to, but something tells me you're a terrific lover, and it intimidates me a little. I'd probably have performance anxiety, then things would get awkward and next thing you know it's all over town. So, no, you're safe on that account." I took a swig of my beer.

While she didn't exactly break out in a belly laugh, she did at least smile. She stole another glance at the mirror, watching the door. "He must be a real studley, the guy you're waiting on."

"One, who says I'm waiting on anyone? And two, if I was, who says it's a guy?"

"Well, you keep watching the door. Plus, women who look like you don't end up in dives like this by choice. Ergo, you're meeting someone. And, as far as you waiting for a woman? That would be wrong on so many different levels from this red-blooded-American-male's point of view. So you just can't be playing for the other team." I stuck my hand out. "I'm Vic."

"Ergo?" She smiled, taking my hand, her grip firm, her skin soft. My heart beat about a hundred times faster at her touch. "Miranda." And I now knew I had the right woman. I felt like a man who hit the lottery jackpot. I honestly didn't think I would find her this quickly.

I considered my next line when two things happened at almost the same time: Miranda slipped off her bar stool, wrapped her arms around my neck and kissed me deeper than any woman ever kissed me before. One hand slid up my neck and into my hair. Being the calm, cool and collected professional I am, I went with it. Like this kind of thing happened to me all the time, I returned the kiss with the same passion, my own hands moving to the small of her back, pulling her tightly against me.

The second thing that happened, just fractions before the kiss, was the door to the bar opened and a man, a Billy Idol wannabe with spiked blond hair and Elvis Presley sneer, stuck his head inside. Acne scars covered his face and it appeared he hadn't had a passing encounter with a shower in some time.

Miranda turned us so her back was to the door, watching him through nearly closed eyes using the mirror. The twerp leered at us for a moment, checked out the Marlboro couple and went back outside, closing the door.

The moment the door closed, Miranda broke off the kiss, picked up her case and a coat lying on the next bar stool, then headed for the far end of the bar into the back room, me one step behind her. If there were any questions about why she kissed me, there wasn't any longer.

The bartender said, "Hey! You can't go back there!" He grabbed for Miranda, but she ducked and eluded his grasp. When I pushed him out of the way, he took a step back and launched a roundhouse right hand that started back somewhere in Illinois.

He quickly learned the biggest difference between shadow boxing and real boxing. Shadows don't hit back. I stepped into the punch, taking the blow on my left shoulder and fired off two quick right hooks to his midsection, followed by a left cross to his chin and then, "Down goes Frazier! Down goes Frazier!"

By the time I got to the back room, Miranda was already out the door.

Chapter Five

Opening the door, I exited the Double D into a short parking lot for deliveries, lit by a powerful floodlight. One side was a dead end, with a dumpster taking up most of the space. A retaining wall followed the length of the alley. The only other thing in sight was a Harley Davidson Fat Boy motorcycle that I guessed belonged to the bartender, and Miranda, peeking around the far corner of the building.

The door closed behind me and I heard a loud snick as the bolt caught. Miranda turned and quickly ran back towards me. "I have to get back inside! Now!" she said, panic in her voice.

"No can do, sister," I said, trying the door knob. "It's locked. What's the problem?"

"The problem is I'll be dead soon if I don't get out of this alley!"

Running past, she began to climb up on the dumpster as the blond twerp came around the corner, sauntering our way. Looking at her, I said, "What? You're worried about this blond reject from the Lollipop Guild?"

Evidently I pissed Blondie off because he picked up the motorcycle and threw it at my head. At. My. Head.

I've spent a lot of time hanging with and tracking down members of the Hell's Angels and happen to know A Fat Boy weighs north of six-hundred pounds. Blondie couldn't have weighed more than a buck fifty, yet the bike flew by me like a Randy Johnson fastball. I ducked just in time and Miranda jumped off the dumpster, as the bike hit the top of it, leaving a huge dent in it and the bike. No doubt the bartender was having a really bad day—though he didn't know it yet.

"Dude, you have to lay off the steroids. It's leading to anger issues. Let me guess," I asked, "Too late for an apology and a group hug?"

Guess so. Growling like some rabid dog, he charged me. This threw me for a loop as most men run away from me, not towards me. Then again, I've never had anyone throw a bike at me, either. As he was crashing into me, I hit him hard with a two-handed blow to the back of his head, trying to end things right then and there. No dice. Lifting me off my feet and slamming me into a dumpster, he knocked the wind out of my sails. Jesus Christ, the shot I gave him would have crippled most men. Yet, all he did was start to laugh.

He said, "Tough bastard, you are. But 'ole Eamon is tougher, don't you think?"

It was all I could do not to start gagging from the stench of his breath as it smelled like he'd been eating road kill for dinner. "First off," I said, "Talking about yourself in the third person points to some severe psychological issues. Second, man, you could use some Tic-Tacs."

I leaned back, then drove forward and struck him in the nose with a fierce headbutt. I heard his nose crunch and break, a smushed lump in the middle of his acne craters. He started giggling and tried headbutting me back, but I shifted my head at the last moment and he struck the side of the dumpster, leaving another huge dent.

I think he would have killed my ass right then and there, but Miranda tried running past him.-Blondie lunged at her, grabbing hold of her hair. A blonde wig came off in his hands as she spun away from him, revealing short red hair the color of a setting sun. In one fluid motion, she opened her case, and instead of a pool stick, her hand emerged holding a long, thin sword, its razor edge glinting in the spill of light from the backdoor bulb.

She made a slashing cut towards his hand, making Blondie jump back. Tossing the wig aside, he began approaching her cautiously, forgetting all about me. "Now Samantha, you want to be careful with that thing, girl. A child such as yourself ought not to be playing with a man's toy." He started dancing a little jig as he talked, trying to cut her off from the open end of the alley, but she continued circling, holding the sword in front of her, keeping him from blocking her escape.

"You took what wasn't yours to take," he chortled. "So they sent old Eamon to bring you back, they did. But they didn't say how or in what condition, don't you know. So if you don't put that pig sticker away, when I do take it from you, well, then I'm going to use it on you a few times, then have me fun with you. Show you what a real man is like."

"Eamon, I swear to God, you pull out your shortcomings and I'll slice it off and shove it down your throat." There was fear on her face, but the sword in her hands remained steady. She kept backing away from him, but he maintained the same pace.

Samantha? I know I'd had my helmet pummeled pretty hard, but what the hell? Guess Miranda wasn't her real name. At the moment, though, her name didn't make any difference. What mattered was that Blondie now had his back to me. Pushing my way to my feet, my back screamed in protest. Sometimes it just doesn't pay to get out of bed.

I don't care what type of freak of nature you are, if you turn your back to me during a fight, I'm going to make you pay. Running a couple of steps I hurled myself in a flying tackle, hitting Blondie square in the back, jack-knifing him right in the middle, with me taking him off his feet. This resulted in his head being thrown backwards. Miranda stepped smoothly to the side, and swung the sword across in a deadly arc. Blondie's scream was cut off as his head went flying from his neck.

Chapter Six

When you separate a man's head from his shoulders, it's messy. The carotid artery will spray a jet of blood rhythmically as the heart continues to pump out the last few beats of life. The body will spasm, while the head drips a bloody trail wherever it lands. It's amazing what you can learn from watching the History Channel.

So imagine my surprise, when, instead of landing on a decapitated body, I found myself landing on a body turning to blackened stone. Bright red veins ran up and down his torso, like embers from a dying fire and the smell of sulfur filled the air. Crashing to the ground, the body disintegrated into a cloud of yellow ash, and his head rolled to a stop next to the retaining wall. Blondie's mouth was open in a frozen scream that would now never end. Kind of a reverse Venus De Milo.

Jumping up and backing away, I dusted off the coating of ash from my bomber jacket, I was beginning to feel like someone had just dropped me in the Twilight Zone. Miranda, or Samantha, or whoever the hell she was, started putting her sword back into its case.

Walking hurriedly up to me, she leaned in and kissed me on the cheek. "I can't thank you enough and I know you have questions, but I really have to go."

She turned and started to head out of the alley, with me following, the feeling of her lips lingering on my cheek. "Hey, wait up. You have to tell me what the hell just happened back here. I mean, this is beyond freaky. You can't just bail on me like this."

She kept walking, talking over her shoulder. "I don't have time. Believe me, the best thing you can do is get out of here and forget you ever met me."

She was going around the corner, when I pulled her back. Shrugging out of my grip, anger flashed in her eyes. She started to say something, until she noticed me put a finger to my lips and make a hush sound. I pointed to J.B. and his two goons, who were just going in the Double D's front door. They'd gotten here much quicker than I expected and

J.B. looked ready to tear somebody's head off. Lucky me.

I said, "The guy you just off'd was sitting with those three in the Escalade parked over there by my car and they were having an in-depth conversation. My guess is it had to be about you."

I told the lie so smoothly. As a bounty hunter, you often have to lie your way into and out of situations. It's part of the job and I usually never give it a second thought. Truth be told, most times its fun. I have a very creative imagination. But when I told this one, I could feel my stomach turn into knots as I could feel my soul sliding further down the slippery slope to Hell.

Waiting until they went inside, she took off running over to her Mercedes, but she wasn't going anywhere. Someone had slashed the tires on her car. I guess Blondie left her a nice 'screw you' parting gift. The other cars in the lot, including mine, were untouched. She started looking around wildly, her face etched in desperation.

Opening the passenger door to my car, I said, "Get in, I'll get you out of here." She looked at me and then at the bar, considering what waited for her inside. "Look lady, you need help and I can provide it. You want to wait for those three to come back out?"

She hesitated a moment longer and then decided to finally hop in my car. I did a quick reverse out of the parking lot, threw the shifter in drive, and slammed the pedal down, tearing out of the parking lot. I made several quick turns, keeping an eye on the rear view mirror. I saw no sign of J.B. or anyone else. My passenger was eyeballing her side mirror intently, watching for the same signs of pursuit. When there was none, she started to relax a bit, but continued to keep a tight grip on her sword case.

"You're pretty good with that thing," I said, nodding to the case.

"My father insisted I study martial arts, starting when I was very young. I had learned how to use a sword after getting my black belt."

"Strike one up for Dad. So, where to?"

She was still watching her mirror. "If you don't mind, just drive for a bit while I think about it."

I did as she asked, taking us on a path over towards I-65, changing directions occasionally. "Care to explain what just happened back there?"

Leaning her head against the window and closing her eyes, she said, "You wouldn't believe me if I told you."

"Lady, I just had a Smurf throw a motorcycle at my head, after which you go all Highlander on his ass and then he turns to stone? Considering my night so far, you might be surprised at what I'd believe. So try me." Glancing at her I could feel my heart catching. I'm guessing there have been wars fought over women who were not half so beautiful. And here I was, in less than twenty-four hours, supposed to hand her over to the Devil.

Opening her eyes she sat staring at me for a long moment, as if sizing me up and trying to decide whether to trust me or not. I waited. Finally, she took a deep breath, and said, "O.K. If you really want to know, the guy back there was a vampire."

I'm not sure what I expected, but this was nowhere near the top of the list. "You mean like Twilight or True Blood? That type of vampire?"

"No. Nothing like them at all. That's all Hollywood made up bullshit." She stopped, struggling with what she should, or shouldn't say next. "Let me ask you something. Do you believe in Heaven and Hell? God and the Devil?"

Before this morning, I thought, I could have cared less. Now, they were both all too real. I said, "As a recovering Catholic, yeah, I guess I do. It's not like I've spent much time thinking about it, but sure. I believe in both. Why do you ask?"

"Here's the deal, O.K.?. When someone is evil, and I mean really, truly evil, after they die, sometimes Satan will offer them a second chance at life on Earth if they'll come back here and do his bidding. But if they die a second time, then their punishment is beyond horrific. Or if they don't do exactly what he asks them to do, they can be punished here, before they are called back to Hell. When they come back here, they don't age. They don't sleep."

"And the only way to kill them is to cut off their heads? Seriously?" I asked.

She shook her head. "That's just the most permanent way. You can burn them and turn them into human bonfires. Or you can bury them deep in the ground or in cement. They aren't dead when you do that, but they're out of the picture. If you chop an arm off, they just keep coming. But cut off their head and they're toast."

She said, more to herself than to me, "I don't believe this. I really, don't believe this. They've sent a goddamned vampire after me?"

She pulled her knees up to her chest, wrapping her arms around them and clung to her sword case. Her dress slipped down her thighs…but I tried not to notice "Look it, I know I sound nuts. But what I'm telling you is the truth. But there's more. And if I die, what I know dies with me. I have to tell someone."

I said, "Lay it on me."

She said, "Alright. Eamon was born in the early 1800's in Ireland. During the Great Famine, he would murder people for their food and that's one of the less offensive things he would do. Children disappeared near any town he lived in. When he couldn't find food to steal, he would eat people. After he died, he got another chance and has been one of Satan's top foot soldiers. Or used to be. Now he's back in Hell where he belongs."

"He said you took something and they want it back. What'd you steal and who is 'they'?"

"The 'what' isn't important." She sat for a long time, gazing out the window, considering her reply. Then said, "The who is the Church of the Light Reclaimed."

"Never heard of them. Who the hell are they?"

"Devil worshippers." She glanced my way, waiting for a reaction, but I continued to drive. "Satan thinks of himself as the Angel of Light, hence the name. He's seeking what he thinks is his rightful place in Heaven, over God. And they're looking for me, and want me bad enough to send a vampire after me." She shivered, and not from the cold.

And not to mention at least two bounty hunters and who the hell else knows what. "Is that why you know so much about vampires, because you're a member?"

She said, "No. Well, I guess you could say that. My father told me about them. And he should know. He's Lucifer's pope."

My jaw dropped, but before I could ask anything else, her hand slid into a coat pocket and took out a cell phone and she started to make a phone call. I could hear a man's voice begin talking as the call went to voicemail. She said, "David, there've been complications. You have to call me back, please." Ending the call, she put her phone away.

"Is David the guy you were waiting for at the bar?"

"No. David's a reporter. He's involved in all this and helped me set up the meeting I was supposed to have tonight, but the guy never showed and I got Eamon instead."

"Who were you supposed to meet?"

"Just a guy David thought could help stop whatever the Church has planned. I'd never met the guy before."

"The vamp called you Samantha. I'm guessing Miranda's not your real name, is it?"

Letting out a another long sigh, she said, "No. It's not. I guess since my cover's blown, what difference does it make? My real name is Samantha." Laying a hand on my arm, she said, "Look, you've been really great helping me like this. But if you're anywhere near me when they catch me, they'll kill you. Once I get a hold of David and make a plan B, you can drop me off at a car rental place and I'll get out of your hair."

The Devil had offered me a deal: find the girl and save my brother's soul. Now I had her and all I had to do was take her to my office and wait until 6 P.M. tomorrow and hand her over. Job complete. I'd gotten lucky. Another five minutes later and Eamon would have taken her and my brother would have been damned for all time. But now that she sat in the seat next to me, I was torn. Not because she was drop dead gorgeous, although that never hurt. It's because I was now just as worried about my own soul as I was my brother's. Would doing this job for Satan see me end up in Hell? Driving, I sat and kept racking my brain for a way out, but couldn't remember any of my classes with Sister Margaret covering this situation. The only thing I did have was a little more time. So I decided playing it out a while longer and seeing what happened would be the best I could do.

I said, "They can try and kill me, but doing it will be a different matter. For what it's worth, seems you need someone to watch your back. I'm good at doing that. Besides, you're a hell of a kisser. Promise me another one when this is over and I'll help you out." I flashed her my best aw shucks grin.

Letting out a short bark of a laugh, she asked, "What do you mean you're good at it? You make a habit of rescuing damsels in distress?"

"Sort of. I work as a bouncer. Before that, a couple of tours with Special Forces in Iraq and Afghanistan. Watching your buddies back is the only way to stay alive. Helping you will be like old times, except you're a hell of a lot cuter than the guys in my unit. So I know how to handle myself in tough situations. Ask Eamon."

While I never worked as a bouncer, I served the time in the Middle East. One day I was just out of range of an exploding IED that unfortunately took the lives of my three closest friends in Iraq. Another day I shot a boy who raised a gun my direction while shouting at me in a language I couldn't understand. The wars, especially the one in Afghanistan, are Hell on Earth. Riding with Samantha I could feel my heartbeat quickening, like it did every time I thought about being over there.

Samantha brought me back to the here and now. "I seem to remember I was the one that cut off his head," she said.

"True, you're the one that turned him into a pigeon stand, but I'm the one that gave you the opportunity. Like I said, you need someone to watch your back. At least things around you aren't boring, and I miss the action. So what do you say?"

She thought about it. "O.K. You're right. I do need the help. I can't do this alone. I can pay you. Name your price."

I waved her off and smiled. "The kiss is payment enough for now," I said. "Let's see how things are in twenty-four hours. Who knows what the future holds?" I was beginning to feel only Heaven knew.

Chapter Seven

"So what next," I asked.

Biting her bottom lip, she thought for a moment and said, "It would sure help if David would call me back."

"If he won't, then let's go to him. Do you know where he lives?"

"Yes. He's renting a small home in Butchertown that backs up to Eastern Cemetery. He told the owners he wanted to write a book about the area."

"Vampires, devil worshipers, cemeteries? What's up with you people?"

She gave me the directions along with a Spock eyebrow raise and we headed that way.

"O.K. How about giving me the low-down on how this reporter fits in? Who does he write for and what's his angle in all of this?"

"The guy's a freelancer for several different Christian magazines and newspapers. About two months ago, he had gotten wind of something the Church was planning called the Exodus Project. He has a source, but all the source could tell him was the Project involved doing something that would hurt Christian schools in the South, while at the same time starting a religious war between Christians and Muslims, and that it would be going down here in Louisville. So he started looking for a way to get inside the Church for more information."

"And he found you. How exactly? Craig's List for Satanists?"

Shrugging one beautiful shoulder she said, "Close enough. I spend a lot of time reading blogs, including some about the Church. He posted on several of them. Over the course of a couple of weeks we struck up a conversation. He had dropped a few hints about the Exodus Project in some emails and it got me curious, so I started nosing around. David and I met a couple of times over the last few weeks."

"How does digging around in Church business square with you being a cheerleader for Satan?" I found myself watching her, her face moving in and out of shadows created by passing street lights and I could feel my heart shifting, my soul slipping.

Shaking her head she said, "I'm hardly a cheerleader. As a matter of fact, I'm an atheist. Or, at least I was. The only reason I'm a member of the Church is because my dad is one. To me, God and the Devil have always been like Santa Claus or the Easter Bunny: figments of the imagination. When I found out my dad worshiped the Devil, I just thought he was weird, you know? Then again, I thought people who believed in God were weird. So when he asked me to help with Church stuff I did. But since I've been poking around, I've discovered some things that have had me questioning everything I thought I knew. Now I do think Satan exists, but I'm not sure God does."

"How can you have one without the other? Yin, Yang, all that bullshit? If the Devil exists then, ergo, God does, too, does he not?"

"Not when one of them is dead," she said. "Look around you: wars, murders, rape, abuse. And what has God done to stop it? Not a damn thing. You see the Devil's fingerprints everywhere. But how about God? Ever since they nailed his Son up on a couple of wooden ties, there's been nothing for at least two-thousand years."

Thinking about what she was saying, it didn't ring true for me. The Devil isn't all powerful and if God was dead, he sure as hell would be the one calling all the shots. And in our brief meeting, Satan seemed pissed as all get out at God. But it's not like I could tell Samantha the truth.

"Well, like I said, I'm a recovering Catholic, but I still believe in the Big Man upstairs. So do you think your dad knows that the church sent a vamp after you?" I asked.

"Nothing happens in that church that he doesn't know about." She rubbed her eyes with the heel of her hands as she tried to stop the tears from falling.

"Wow. That's harsh." I thought about my own dad, who had to track me down on some of my wild nights when I was a teenager out on the town. My mother would be worried sick. To think a father would send something like Eamon after his own daughter made him one royal son of a bitch.

We had a few more minutes until we reached David's house. "If you don't mind my asking, can you tell me more about the Church and about this Exodus Project? What kind of things have you found out?"

Being so direct and pushing her was a gamble. But I could tell she felt betrayed by her father. And I needed to know as much about what was going on as possible if I was to save my brother. The gamble paid off. Whether from desperation, stress, or a sense of betrayal, after a moment's hesitation, the dam broke.

"I had nosed around my dad's office and one thing I found out is that the Church has an enemies list. The file's a list of people or organizations that the Church feel are a threat and what actions to take against them.

"There's also a complete background on several "fixers" the Church uses. Eamon is one, or was. I'd met him once or twice and dad had told me about him being a vampire and all, but I just laughed it off. I mean, come on? The first time I read the file, I thought it was somebody's idea of a joke. Vampires? I mean, get real. Then I did a search on the names of the people they supposedly sent him after and they all turned up either dead or missing.

"Dad also told me about ways to slow vampires down or kill them, in case they get out of control. That's why I was carrying around my sword. I didn't think they'd really send one after me, but I thought I should be ready just in case. The Church punished one vampire by burying her in cement under a new baseball stadium. Vampires don't need to breathe or eat, so she will be there for an eternity. And she evidently hated sports. They learned not to bury them in dirt because they'll eventually dig their way out."

"Sucks to be her," I said. This conversation made me start to understand how Alice must have felt when she dropped down the rabbit hole. I prodded her to continue. "What were you able to learn about this Exodus Project itself?"

"Unfortunately, not much. I just know that whatever it is, it will happen soon. My dad may be a big muckety-muck, but I'm not. People started noticing I was asking a lot of questions. So I cooled it for a bit. Then one night I came back to my place and could tell it had been searched. There was nothing for them to find because I'd been careful, but still. It both scared me to death and pissed me off. So I took off."

Took off with something the Church and Satan wanted very badly, I thought. I could sense I was getting closer to the truth of the matter. I needed to find out what she stole. Perhaps I could use what she'd taken as leverage for my brother's soul without actually serving her up on a silver platter.

We were now in the eastern part of Louisville, near Beargrass Creek.

The area is called Butchertown because back in the day, the creek had been lined up one side and down the other with slaughterhouses and butcher shops. They would throw the scraps and what not into the creek and just let it take all the crap to the Ohio River. I can only imagine the smell of the place on a hot August day.

Butchertown is home to two cemeteries, Eastern Cemetery and right next door to that, Cave Hill Cemetery. Cave Hill is Louisville's crown jewel of cemeteries with many of the city's dignitaries buried in and around the hills. It's wonderfully maintained and surrounded by a brick wall with razor wire on top to keep out unwanted visitors. People take tours of Cave Hill Cemetery. It's on the National Register of Historic Places. It's beautiful and peaceful. I even have relatives buried there.

Eastern Cemetery is nothing like Cave Hill. Home to many of the city's past prominent black leaders, it's also home to one of the city's darkest secrets. It was discovered that since the 1920's, the people who were running the cemetery had been burying multiple corpses in the same graves. Not only that, but they were mixing the cremated remains of different people into the same boxes. I would hate to find out my Great Aunt Edna was buried with somebody else's Uncle Hubert.

The cemetery has been largely abandoned since the late 80's when it was learned they had buried nearly forty-eight thousand people in sixteen-thousand graves. Tombstones were desecrated, records were lost. Word around town is some guy decided on his own to mow the grass there because no one else would. It breaks my heart to think of all the loved ones that were not buried with the respect they had earned in life.

We turned onto David's street and pulling to the curb. I stopped. "Which house is it?" I asked.

"The last one at the end, on the right."

I spent a few moments getting a feel for the neighborhood. The cool air made for a pleasant night. Most of the houses up and down the street had cars in the driveway or parked in front. Putting the car back in drive, I drove slowly down the street and watched for anything out of place, but didn't see anything. When we got to David's house, there were lights on in the back and a car in the driveway.

"Looks like someone's home. Is that his car?"

"Yeah, the green Hyundai."

I kept on going and then turned at the end of the street, circling the block. "Call him back."

Pulling out her phone, she did so. After a moment, she looked at me and shook her head. No answer. "He knew my meeting was tonight and told me to call as soon as it was over. I don't know why he's not answering. Why aren't we stopping?"

My years of busting perps had my Spidey senses tingling at full blast. Phoenix Hill Tavern was across the street from the entrance to Eastern Cemetery. Easing into the lot, I took the time and backed into a space.

I parked the car and sat back in my seat, I said, "Let me ask you a few things first, starting with how many people knew about your meeting at the Down and Dirty?"

We could hear the music pounding from inside the tavern, people having fun letting their hair down on a Friday night. While across the street, the cemetery waited quietly, with a clientele that had left the party a long time ago.

She took a deep breath. "Just David, me, and the guy I was meeting." She paused. "Which means I have a problem."

I thought about it. It was unlikely that Eamon found out about her meeting the same way I did, as I couldn't picture the vamp locking the door behind him when he left. And even if he was working with J.B., I doubt he could get there that quickly. Which left one other option.

"Yep. Sure seems like someone might have sold you out. Sounds like David has a vested interest in what you're doing, so that makes me think your date tonight set you up."

She waved the comment off dismissively. "No. He wouldn't. And that's the real problem. Have you ever heard of the Hand of God?"

"Sorry, I can't say that I have. Then again, if it isn't on the side of a beer bottle, I might not have anyway. Enlighten me."

"David told me about this guy that does God's dirty work here on Earth. The Hand of God is…special. Kind of like God's James Bond with a license to kill."

She continued, "People tend to forget that in the Old Testament, God had no problems punishing the wicked with extreme violence. Noah's flood, the nuking of Sodom and Gomorrah, closing the Red Sea on Pharaoh's army. Piss God off and the penalties could be steep. This guy deals out the same type of punishment, just quieter and on a smaller scale."

My kind of guy. More than once I wish I had the power to dish out the ultimate punishment on some douche bag. The thing stopping me is I don't like bars I can't walk out of, and prison is not a place I want to end up in.

"And that's who you were meeting?" I asked.

"Yes. So there is zero chance that the Hand of God would be working with the Church of the Light Reclaimed. Her eyes filled with concern and not a little fear. "I have a bad feeling about all this, Vic. I worked for weeks to set that meeting up. For him not to have shown is beyond bad. And for David not to answer his phone is even worse."

She didn't have to say more. I said, "O.K. That brings us back to how they found out where you were going to be. It may be David had no choice in giving you up, which is why I didn't pull into his driveway. Here's what you and I are going to do. His house backs up to the cemetery. So let's you and I take a little stroll and approach his house from the rear and see what we can see."

Nodding, she got out carrying her case. I walked around to her side of the car. I glanced around to make sure we were more or less alone and then unlocked the glove box, took out my gun and slipped the holster clip on my belt, making sure it was covered by my jacket.

"You need to use that thing much as a bouncer?" she asked.

"You can't imagine how many drunken boozers I toss out on an average night that wait in the parking lot to get a piece of me when I leave. I show them this and they back off. It's why I'm off tonight. I got into it with a few guys and my boss suggested I take the rest of the night off and cool it a bit."

Liar, Liar, pants on fire, kept running through my mind, with the image of my body melting from my bones coming along for the ride. I have a great poker face, but in this case I didn't need it. Samantha either believed my line of bull shit or she simply didn't care, with bigger worries on her mind, as she never blinked at the explanation. As for me, I knew damn well if anyone else threw something large at me, I was going to blow them away, whether it stopped them or not.

Chapter Eight

Crossing the street and heading into the cemetery, we left Phoenix Hill Tavern behind. A large, bright full moon, kind enough to light our path, meant there was no need for a flashlight, even though I keep one in a zipped pocket inside my jacket along with the lock picks and a few other tools of the trade, like a small can of mace.

We walked down a long path between rows of headstones, many of them knocked to the ground or with the tops of some of the more ornate ones vandalized. The grass had not been mowed in some time and it was like I could feel the outrage of those laid to rest at Eastern Cemetery. Guess the volunteer mower had given up the ghost as well.

It only took about five minutes to reach the back of Dave's rental property. Finding a hole in the chain link fence, we were soon standing in the deeper shadows of an oak tree and spent the next several minutes watching the house. The rear of the house featured a screened-in back porch. We could see a light on in a back room that Samantha said was the kitchen. But the only window had the shade drawn, the blind glowing yellow in the night.

We quietly made our way across the backyard and onto the porch, opening the screen door slowly. We could hear voices inside the house and we moved over to the window. There was a small sliver of space between the shade and the sill, and I took a quick look inside.

There were three men in the kitchen and I could pick out David right away. Not because one looked more like a reporter than the other two. It was because I knew he was most likely the one with his torso and arms duct taped to a kitchen chair, with a dish towel in his mouth and two fingers missing from his left hand, dripping a steady stream of blood. Well, the fingers weren't really missing; they were lying on the kitchen floor, where the dweeb with the garden shears let them fall after cutting them off his hand.

The man with the shears was tall and young, with scruffy hair and a beard with several days growth. He was dressed in a James Taylor T-shirt and jeans and looked like the kind of guy you would find playing guitar in a coffee house--as long as you could look past the whole bloody garden shears cutting fingers off part. He also had a 9 millimeter stuck in the back waistband of his pants.

The other man looked like George Clooney, with movie star good looks and a deep tan, a comfortable six feet tall. He was dressed in what looked like a very expensive suit and was clearly the man in charge. He leaned back against the kitchen counter, his hands clasped loosely in front of him.

I pointed to Samantha to take a look, but to keep quiet when she did so. She nodded she understood, then eased to where she could look through the window. Her eyes went wide and her hands flew to cover her mouth as she stifled a scream.

After a moment she regained her composure and placing her mouth next to my ear, she said, "The man in the suit is Preston Deveraux. He works for my dad. He's another one of the Church fixers. The other is a low-life scumbag named Kevin Hall. He does odd jobs at the church headquarters."

I was struggling to concentrate on what she was telling me, with my body paying more attention to the feel of her breath in my ear and the way her hand rested on my neck.

Swallowing hard before putting my mouth next to her ear, I asked, "Is either one of them a vampire?"

She shook her head no. That was good news, at least. I like it when things I shoot will stay on the ground instead of getting back up and trying to kick my ass. I was glancing back through the gap when Deveraux opened his trap and started talking.

"All right, Mr. Mangus. We're going to try this again. When we run out of fingers I'll have my associate pull down your pants and start cutting off other things. He's going to take the rag out of your mouth and you're going to answer my questions. Do you understand me?"

David raised his head, with effort, and nodded. He appeared to be around fifty or sixty years old, with a round face and closely cropped gray hair. He was breathing hard, his face covered in sweat.

Deveraux asked, "What's the Exodus Project?"

Hall removed the dish towel and David said, his voice strained, "It's a....it's a planned attack on Christian schools using a computer virus," he stammered. Tears streaked his bloodied face and his body shook in pain.

I could feel my anger rising and pulled my gun from its holster. Samantha watched me do this, opened her case and then took out her sword. When I raised an eyebrow, she whispered, "It works on regular people just as well as vampires." She got no argument from me. Any port in a storm and any weapon in a dogfight.

"And who told you about the Exodus Project, Mr. Mangus? And remember, I know the answers to most of these questions already. One more lie and the night will be over for you. And then I'll leave here, drive to your daughter Linda's house in Atlanta and see what she knows."

He looked up in panic at the mention of his daughter.

"That's right, Mr. Mangus. We know quite a bit about you. Cooperate with me now and we'll leave you as you are. You won't be able to play the piano anymore, but at least you'll be alive."

Fat chance on that one, David. I could see in his eyes that he felt the same, but still, he answered. "Leave my…leave my daughter alone," he stuttered. "I'll tell you what you want to know." He paused for a moment, in significant pain, but continued. "Rebecca Thomas contacted me with information on Exodus. She said the Church of the Light Reclaimed was planning an attack on Christian schools in the South with a computer virus. That's all she knew. And that's all I know. I swear!"

I looked at Samantha and mouthed the name Rebecca Thomas and she mouthed back no clue.

Kevin Hall was whistling a tune and after a moment I realized it was *Sunshine on My Shoulders*. Never thought anyone could make John Denver sound creepy, but ole' Kevin pulled it off.

Deveraux asked, "One last question, Mr. Mangus. You contacted someone in the Church. Who was it?"

David swallowed hard a couple of times, then said in a near whisper, "Samantha. Samantha Tyler." He dropped his head to his chest and started to sob.

Samantha, eyes closed, slowly shook her head back and forth. .

Deveraux moved in front of David. He bent over and lifted up his chin, so that he and David were looking eye to eye. "Where is she now, Mr. Mangus?"

David stared back and said, "I, I have no clue. Really. I don't know."

Preston Deveraux stood up straight and took a couple of steps back. He looked at Kevin, then nodded at David. I knew what that meant. Moving to the door and trying the knob, I found it was unlocked, so I opened it and stepped into the kitchen, Samantha right behind me, sword raised.

"I'm right here, you son of a bitch!" she shouted.

I pointed my gun at the two men, while using my free hand to hold Samantha back. I knew she wanted nothing more than to run both of them through, and I had no problem with her doing so. But I didn't want her between me and the two men when the shit hit the fan.

If Preston Deveraux was surprised at our entrance, you would never have known it. He looked like someone just walked in and asked him what time it was. A half-smile creased his face as he nonchalantly leaned back on the counter. He raised his hands out to his side, showing he was unarmed. Kevin, on the other hand, jumped and started to reach for his gun.

I said, in my best Danny Glover voice, "I don't want to kill you, and you don't want to be dead, but if your hand moves another inch, that's what's going to happen."

Kevin said, "Mr. Deveraux, I think I can take him." Licking his lips, he moved a fraction more towards his gun. Deveraux just looked at him with a blank stare, watching, but saying nothing.

I felt like I was in a Clint Eastwood western. And I knew how this was going to end. And then it did. Kevin made a quick move for his weapon, but he wasn't nearly as fast as he thought he was. Before he could even get a grip on his 9, I had, for the second time in just the last few hours, shot a man. This time, things happened the way they were supposed to.

The bullet struck Kevin fractions of an inch above the bridge of his nose, throwing him back against the counter, then his lifeless body collapsed to the floor. Blood and brain matter made a weird looking pattern on David's tiled kitchen backsplash. As his head exploded. I wasn't sure, but I could swear I could see a butterfly. David, for his part, just kept saying, "Oh my God, oh my God" over and over and thrashing around on his kitchen chair. The only move Deveraux made was to cross his legs at the ankles, while keeping his hands out to his sides.

Smiling at me, he said, "You just can't find good help these days. Stupid is as stupid does." Turning his attention to Samantha, he said, "How are you, beautiful?"

"Fuck you, Preston." Moving over to David, she tried calming him down. Searching around the kitchen and finding a knife on the counter, she started cutting him free of the duct tape.

I knew I should be feeling some level of guilt at what I'd just done, but I didn't. In truth, I didn't feel anything at all. During my years in the sandpits of the Middle East, I killed dozens of men. And back then all I could muster was a mental shrug of the shoulders. This, for me, was no different. I've laid in bed many nights wondering if my moral compass pointed to nowhere. In this case, I'd warned him. So, he got what he deserved. But deep down inside, my lack of remorse bothered me a hell of a lot more than the killing.

"We've been looking for you, Samantha. Your father is very worried about you," Deveraux said.

"I'll just bet he is." The sarcasm in her voice was obvious.

"Why don't you introduce me to your new friend?" He looked at me and said, "And you are?"

"No one of consequence," I replied. I made sure to keep my gun leveled right at his chest. Over the years I've become a good judge of who is and isn't dangerous. Deveraux struck me as more dangerous than a bed of Eastern Kentucky rattlers.

"Kevin would surely disagree with you. But no matter. Let me make you an offer. You help me return Samantha to her father and we will pay you a finder's fee."

"A finder's fee? Sorry friend, while you may be a looker, I prefer the redhead, thank you very much. You know what I mean? I think you do." I gave it my best Elvis drawl, but Deveraux wasn't overly impressed.

Samantha, after cutting David away from his chair, began wrapping his hand in a clean towel. Looking at me she said, "We have to get David to a hospital, like now."

I said, "Let's call the cops. They can handle things from here. I have you and David as witnesses for the shooting. So let them take over."

"We can't. No cops. We have to get David medical treatment, but no cops. No way." She said this with a strong shake of her head.

"Why the hell not? You want to put pressure on the Church, and this will sure as hell do that."

Deveraux spoke up, "She doesn't want the cops because she doesn't want them to find out what she's done. Isn't that right, Samantha?"

Looking back and forth between the two of them, I asked, "And what is it you're claiming she did?"

Deveraux smiled. "Not much. Only a little matter of the theft of thirty million dollars."

Chapter Nine

Samantha kept her gaze locked on me as I thought about someone stealing thirty million dollars. I could now understand why Satan, the Church and a billion other people might be looking for her if it was true she'd stolen the money. And since I have always been nothing if not direct, I asked her.

I gave a low whistle. "So, did you steal it?"

"Yes." Walking over to a cabinet and staying clear of Deveraux, she got out a bowl and used another clean wash towel to pick up David's fingers, putting them in the bowl. She then got ice out of the fridge and covered the fingers with the cubes.

I couldn't even fathom what having that much money would be like. Not to mention what it would take to have the balls to steal that much money. You take a couple of thousand and maybe not much happens. You steal thirty million and you can bet your sweet ass the ones you stole it from would be hunting you night and day.

Helping David to his feet and then picking up her sword, Samantha stood facing me and waited.

I smiled and said, "You go, girl. Thirty million? Sweet."

Deveraux cleared his throat and said, "Let me up my offer, since you hold the gun. Turn Samantha over to me, help us recover the money, and we will pay you a million dollars. What do you say?"

This guy was starting to royally piss me off. "You know what Preston? May I call you Preston?"

"By all means."

"Preston, I don't know what pisses me off more. That you think I could be bought or that you think I'm that damn stupid. I mean, after all, as you pointed out, I have the gun. Why would I settle for a million from you when I got thirty million standing right there?"

I could see Samantha tensing, so I continued, "But it doesn't matter. I don't need your money or hers. I've never been much of a materialistic kind of guy. The little lady needs help, and I'm giving it to her. Besides, my daddy told me never trust a man with a spray on tan."

All pretense of being friendly disappeared as he said, "Then you're a dead man, you and the reporter both."

"Yeah, yeah, yeah, blah, blah, blah. Have a seat." I waved him over to the chair David had been sitting in and told him to put his hands behind his back. Keeping my gun on him the whole time, I had Samantha duct tape his hands to the chair, then his chest.

I had to give it to the guy. He looked like a man sitting down to have a cup of coffee at Starbucks without a care in the world. He said, "There are forces at work here of which you have no clue. Powers beyond your comprehension, which will all turn their attention to you, once we have Samantha back."

"Yeah? You mean like vampires?"

Deveraux lost his poker face, for just a moment, as an expression of surprise flew across his features, before it returned to casual indifference.

I said, "You must mean Eamon. I met him earlier this evening. You won't get another chance to see him until you get to Hell. But when you do ask him how things are working out for him, since he's dead. Again."

"My, my. It seems I may have underestimated you. Killing a vampire? Bravo."

"Technically, Samantha killed him. But I wore him down for her first before she used her razor and then--" I made a slashing motion across my throat.

Samantha rolled her eyes, and said, "Jeez. What a crock. I had him right where I wanted him, you were just getting in my way."

"Keep on dreaming, sister." David was starting to sway on his feet, so I holstered my gun and took him by the elbow. "Let's get you to a hospital because, man, you don't look too good."

"You should kill me now," said Deveraux. "Leaving me alive is a mistake you can't afford to make. I'll hunt you down and peel the skin from your body and then feed it to you if you leave me alive." The really scary thing is, I could tell he meant it. Both the part about me killing him and the part about hunting me down.

I said, "I don't think you're quite getting the hang of this whole the-tables-are-turned thing. You're supposed to be begging for us not to kill you. The part about peeling my skin thing was good. I would keep pulling the T.V. bad guy card, maybe throw in how I'm going to regret this, that I'll regret the day I was born. Things like that."

He said, "I've been promised a special place by my Lord, the Angel of Light, by his side when he ascends to Heaven. Kill me now and I'll take Eamon's place. Either way, alive or dead, I'll be rewarded. Kill me now and I'll be even more powerful."

I laughed. "Obi-Wan Kenobi you are not."

I started David towards the front of the house, with Samantha returning to the porch and picking up her case, then grabbing the bowl full of fingers.

Deveraux was smiling again. "See you soon, Samantha. Enjoy your freedom and the money while you can. You won't have either for long."

I asked David for his car keys and he pointed to the counter. I picked them up and headed to the front door. I was reaching for the doorknob when I heard car doors open and then shut in the driveway.

"Speaking of tables turning," said Deveraux, "that would be the cavalry."

Four men, dressed in coveralls, were standing next to a white panel van. When they started towards the front door, we made a beeline for the back door.

Deveraux said, "One last chance, friend, to-"

He never finished the sentence because I picked up a wooden cutting board from David's kitchen counter and whacked him hard upside the head, stunning him.

"Jesus, but that man was getting on my nerves." Neither David nor Samantha complained about my method of silencing Deveraux, with both the former Satanist and the Christian keeping quiet.

We made our way out the back door, quickly through the yard to the hole in the fence, and into the cemetery. David was moaning softly under his breath, and I couldn't blame him. There could be no doubt the brutality of the evening would stay with him for the rest of his life.

I asked him, "We heard you mention the name of your source, Rebecca Thomas. Who is she, because you need to call and warn her. After we drop you off at the hospital, we can go pick her up."

I could just make out a couple strolling down the main drag of the cemetery, stopping before they reached us to suck face. Couples sometimes used the cemetery for a little privacy when things got too hot for Phoenix Hill, despite the creepiness factor. Some chicks just dig cemeteries.

Using his good hand, he searched for and then found a cell phone in his pants pocket and flipped it open. Typing in a number he said, "The Church has a computer guru named Lincoln Townsend. Rebecca is both Townsend's maid and mistress. He mentioned the Exodus Project to her during pillow talk. He likes to get high after they have sex and he let something slip one night while high as a kite. It scared the living bejesus out of her. She had read some columns I'd written and contacted me." Hitting the send button, he raised the phone to his ear.

I asked, "Why not go to the police? Did she steal thirty million, too?"

"She was afraid no one would believe her."

David frowned at the couple as we walked by them, their make out session getting more intense, the two of them moaning in pleasure. I just shook my head. The man was wearing a London Fog style overcoat and a fashion sharp fedora hat. The woman had her hands under the man's coat and I resisted the urge to yell out, "Hand check."

In hindsight, it would have been a good idea. As we passed them, the couple broke their embrace, and the woman spun and jammed an ice pick she was holding under her partner's coat, in at the base of David's skull, up and into his brain.

Stiffening, he collapsed like a rag doll, dropping the phone onto the gravel path. He went from being tortured, with seemingly no hope of being saved, to his rescue like a gift from God, only to have his life snuffed out in an instant—and not even knowing how or why. Life can be such a bitch. A cynic would wonder if Samantha was right and God was dead when things like this happen.

Catching the move out of the corner of my eye, I spun around just as the man pulled out his own ice pick and attempted to stab me in my neck. I did a contortion move any yoga instructor would be proud of, seized the man's wrist with my right hand, pulling him forward and then slightly past me. I drove my left hand through the man's elbow, shattering it, with the arm bending nearly back upon itself.

He howled in pain, dropping the ice pick. I started to turn back towards the woman, who had pulled her weapon out of David's gray matter, but I knew I would not be fast enough to stop her from using me like a human pincushion.

Thankfully all that martial arts training Samantha endured paid off as she spun in a circle kick, taking out the woman's legs and then smashing her elbow into the woman's nose as she fell to the ground.

Samantha stomped the hand holding the ice pick with the pointed end of her four inch heels and the woman screamed.

I have to give the man an A for effort, as he tried grabbing me with his free hand. But considering he was of average height and weight, and down to one good arm, he found out that trying to go after me was a very poor decision on his part. I blocked his hand to the side, took a step closer and picking him up by the neck and crotch, lifted him off the ground and slammed him down onto the closest headstone. I heard his back break and I let him slide off the headstone and onto the ground. His bad guy days were now over, unless he planned to terrorize the world from a wheelchair.

I turned to find Samantha kicking the holy hell out of the female side of the Ice Pick Lovers. The woman tried to curl up into a fetal position, this time moaning with pain, instead of pleasure, with each kick. I wrapped my arms around her and lifted her away, as she thrashed trying to get out of my grip to keep punishing the fallen woman. It took a few minutes, but she got herself under control and I sat her back onto her feet, letting her go.

I looked at Phoenix Hill, which was about a hundred yards off, and could see no indication that anyone noticed what had transpired in Eastern Cemetery. Life went on at the tavern, with the death and destruction taking place just a short way into the darkness going unnoticed.

I stepped over David, who was now, I had to guess, strumming the harps and floating on the clouds in Heaven, and picked up his phone. "Hello? Miss Thomas, are you there?"

A very frightened woman asked, "Who is this, what's happening? Where's David?"

"Listen, my name is Victor and I'm a friend of David's. I don't have time to explain, but you're in serious danger. The Church knows who you are and that you're David's source. They'll be sending people your way as soon as they find out where you live, if they haven't already. You have to get out of there and I mean now."

There was a very long pause and I thought she'd hung up.

"Hello? Hello?"

She finally answered me. "How do I know you're not with the Church and just trying to flush me into the open? And tell me what's happened to David?"

"I'm sorry. David's dead. The Church got to him. And there's no way for me to convince you that we're not with the Church. But if you don't listen to me, they'll find you and kill you. He was forced to tell them who his source was before he died, and he named you. So you need to get to a safe place where the Church can't get to you. If you need protection, tell me where you're at, or where we can meet you, and I'll make sure you're safe."

"I don't have a way to leave," she wailed. "I loaned my sister my car for the night!"

"Then go to a neighbor or somewhere near your house that's a public place."

"You don't understand, I live out in the middle of nowhere. I have a small cottage on a farm where I used to work. What am I going to do?"

"O.K. I'll come get you. I'm a big guy wearing a black bomber jacket and I'll be driving a red Chevelle. I'll have a friend with me, and she has red hair. If you see any other car or any other people come to your door, then head somewhere out onto the farm and call us. We called a cell phone, right?"

"Yes. But please hurry." She gave me directions to the farm which was about twenty minutes from us.

"We're on our way." I ended the call.

Samantha knelt in the gravel, stroking David's hair as his eyes stared up at nothing. Tears streamed down Samantha's face. "What do we do with David?" The surrounding tombstones remained silent so I answered.

"Not a damn thing." I looked back towards David's house and I could see movement in the shadows. It would seem Satan's cavalry had figured out how we had made our escape. "I'm sorry Samantha, but if we don't get to Rebecca's first, she's a goner. So we have to get moving and fast."

Samantha looked at me pleadingly. "We can't just leave him here, Vic, we can't."

"We can and we are." I took her by an arm and hauled her to her feet. "His soul has taken the escalator up to Heaven. His body means nothing to him anymore. Now come on, let's go."

She nodded and wiped her eyes with the sleeve of her coat. Then she kicked the Ice Pick Lover one more time for good measure and we took off.

Chapter Ten

As we got closer to exiting the cemetery, I could see my Chevelle in the parking lot with Winston Reynolds leaning against the back bumper, watching the front door to Phoenix Hill.

Winston was one of J.B.'s two helpers. A former linebacker for the University of Louisville football team, he worked out hard to maintain his physique. A black man in his early twenties, he was considered J.B.'s protégé because of his reputation as a smart and quick learner. He's also one of the guys I saw walking into the Double D with J.B. How the hell they tracked us here I had no idea and no time to figure out.

I whispered to Samantha, "Recognize him? That's one of the guys who was after you back at the bar. The other two must be inside looking for us. Wait here on the sidewalk and let me take care of this."

She did as I asked. Their Cadillac Escalade was parked a few spots down from mine, so I strolled over to it, took out my pocket knife, and slowly used it to let the air out of the SUV's back right tire.

Winston continued to watch the front door with his arms crossed, looking bored. I walked around the Escalade, and around Winston's blind side.

I asked, "Hey buddy, got a light?"

He turned his head to look in my direction and I hit him hard, right in the jaw, knocking him off my car, then pressed my attack, hitting him a couple of more times. There were several people in the parking lot and they came over to watch us go at each other.

I have to give Winston credit. He put up a good fight, but my sucker punch gave me the advantage as I'd rung his bell and his reflexes and timing were slow. In short order he was on the ground, not moving.

I ran to the Chevelle, got in, fired her up and pulled out of the lot, stopping long enough to throw the door open for Samantha to jump in, then tore off as soon as she had her door shut. I could see the men in the coveralls jogging towards the cemetery entrance as we zoomed by. I flipped them off with a smile as we accelerated into the night.

Samantha turned in her seat to watch them as we drove away. The men waited a couple of heartbeats, one of them talking on a phone, and then they ran back the way they had come.

"I don't understand. How could those guys at the bar find us so quickly?" she asked.

"I have no earthly idea." And I didn't. "If they're working with Eamon, then the Church must have had them drive over to David's house. But why on Earth they were checking for us in the tavern, I have no clue. Who the hell knows? Problem is, they now know what I'm driving, and we sure as hell can't go back and get your car."

I now had to wonder if the lie I told her was closer to the truth than I realized. It was possible that Satan had put J.B. in touch with Deveraux and that's how they found us, but I didn't think so. Maybe they had sent out word they were looking for my car and someone called and told them it was parked at Phoenix Hill Tavern and that was how they tracked us down, but right then I didn't have time to worry about it.

I took several random turns, but like earlier, could see no pursuit. Not yet, at least.

Samantha put her head back on the head rest and then clenched her fists. Her entire body shook as she fought back tears. "Those goddamned sons of bitches. Before they kill me, I'll make them pay for what they did to David. I swear it."

"First, we're not going to let them kill you. Second, that's why you stole the money, wasn't it? Not to get rich, but to hurt the Church. You wanted to hit them where it hurts, by taking off with their cash."

She nodded. "I couldn't find out exactly what the Exodus Project was, but by what little I could find out from my dad, I could tell it was going to cost the Church a lot of money. I figured if I drained the accounts, they wouldn't be able to go through with the plan, no matter what it is. It was the only way I could think of to slow them down."

"Couldn't they just get more money?"

"No. They're not like a regular church, with a lot of different donors. They don't have as many people to get money from, so losing this much money really puts a hurt on their plans. They can replace the money eventually, but not right away. I helped my dad with the books. He didn't trust anyone else. I knew in which accounts the money was being held and what his passwords were to access them."

I realized that was why Satan wanted her found. He wanted to keep the Exodus Project on schedule, and to do that, they had to find Samantha and the money. Now I had to figure out how to make that information work for me, to save my brother. For the first time all night, I had hope I could free my brother's soul without having to turn over Samantha.

"You also knew it would make you a target. Risky move."

"Yeah, but I thought that my father being who he was would protect me, you know? And so far it has, but look what's happening to the people around me. David's dead now because of what I did. They almost killed you as well."

I shook my head. "David was a big boy and knew what he was getting involved in. He came to you, after all. But you poke a hornets' nest with a stick; there's a good chance you'll get stung. I'm sure he never thought he would pay with his life, but at least he knew where his ticket is punched to end up now that his life is over. As for me, it'll take more than a pointed stick to take me out."

Samantha stopped shaking and took a couple of deep breaths. "I'll say it again, God is dead. If people like David are working to save Christian school kids, how could God let something like this happen to him? Tortured? Murdered? No way, Vic. God's dead."

I would have loved to have argued for the home team, but what could I say? That this was just a test for people like her and me? A woman that didn't believe in either God or Satan until recently? A man like me, who just a couple of hours ago was a casual believer who really couldn't have cared less?

Frankly, I had no clue why God let things like this happen. My parish priest taught us that there wasn't always a reason why things happened. Earthquakes, floods, hurricanes and the like were part of life. No one knows when they'll be called home. Or to the basement, for that matter. It makes the free will that men and women have even more important.

We all have a choice whether we believe in God or not, and you don't want to get caught with your shorts around your ankles when your time to go before the Almighty comes around.

But I knew I couldn't convince her, right at this moment, one way or the other. So I let the question go and changed the subject. "What I don't get is all this is over a computer virus? Just how in God's name is this supposed to start a religious war? This makes no sense to me. I mean, I've had a virus before on my computer and wanted to kill the guy who designed it, but I wouldn't actually kill him. Maybe rough him up a little if I actually caught him, but a religious war?"

"No clue," she said. "Then again Muslims got really ticked when that newspaper guy drew a cartoon of Mohammed and they wanted to kill him for it. Remember that? But the information we have says the attacks will come against Christian schools, not Muslim schools. All I do know is I want to make them pay. And I plan on starting with my father.

"When this crap is over, I plan on holding a press conference. He and the Church do everything in the dark and I'll drag them into the media spotlight and that will ruin them. My father lives in Philadelphia, where he is considered to be a 'Pillar of the Community.' Wait until they find out he has a hand in murdering people and planning attacks on school kids. This time Cy Tyler will be on every news channel and on the cover of every magazine in the country, if not the world, but for a different reason. That's the way you hurt my father and the Church."

"Cy Tyler? You mean Congressman Cy Tyler, the right wing conservative nut job who wants to outlaw nearly anything that's fun in this country and is the darling of the Christian Right? You're telling me that he's a Satanist?

"One and the same, and not just any Satanist, but *the* Satanist."

"Huh. Well, if you do that, your life will never be the same. Until the day they put you in the ground, you'll be known as "That Girl." Can you imagine what it would've been like being Hitler's daughter? You'll get to find out if you shove your dad and the Church into the light."

"So what? You think I should just keep my mouth shut? You want to just let them get away with it? Is that it? Give me a break." She did not try to hide her contempt.

"Hell no. I just think you should consider doing it differently, is all. Just because you sucked at trying to create a new identity for yourself the first time doesn't mean you shouldn't try it again. I know people that can help with that kind of thing. And once you have a new identity, leak things to the media and the powers that be. You can do just as much damage to the Church by lobbing bombs from the shadows, but avoid standing in front of a group of microphones. It gives you a chance at a normal life. You do it your way, and you're hosed."

She didn't say yes and she didn't say no. As a matter of fact, for the rest of the drive, she didn't say anything. As much as my life had been turned upside down, I could only imagine what she was going through. It's one thing to know your father was leading a double life. But to then find out he's an out and out royal bastard is even worse.

We drove the twenty miles out of Louisville into the countryside. Rebecca's cottage was off Covered Bridge Road, a long, winding road taking us farther and farther from civilization. I knew the area because as a kid I used to go to a Boy Scout camp not far from the farm she was living on. There used to be an actual covered bridge, but it was replaced some years ago by a new, wider, modern concrete bridge which screamed progress if not atmosphere. Not only that, there was a rumor devil worshippers used to hold meetings in a field just down from the bridge. Groups of kids would camp out on the hill overlooking the field, watching for them, but they never actually saw them. I would have bet everything I owned devil worshippers, in any great numbers, didn't exist. And it seems I would have lost the bet.

We found the driveway turn off with some difficulty, having gone past it once and backtracking, before finally seeing it, tucked under overhanging oak trees. The farm itself straddled a long ridge, with a beautiful view of the Louisville skyline lit up in the distance. Old growth trees surrounded the property, with many of them having lost their leaves now that we were in the first week of November.

The cottage was situated about a half mile from the main house, down a dirt road with two tire track ruts along its length. We pulled to the end of the drive, parked and got out. The home was small, but well maintained, with neatly trimmed hedges in front and a rose garden off to one side. A creek ran through the back of the property.

I could see a curtain move as we approached the door, then drop back into place. I knocked and the door opened a fraction, showing an attractive woman who appeared to be in her mid-thirties.

"Miss Thomas?" I asked.

She looked past us to see if she could see anyone else. When she didn't, she asked, "I still don't know if I should trust you."

"Look, Miss Thomas, if I wanted to do you harm, I would have kicked the door in and this would be over. This is Samantha. She was working with David. Did he tell you about her?"

"Not by name. He told me he had someone on the inside he was working with, but not who it was."

She opened the door and motioned for us to come in.

I said, "We don't have much time. We have to get out of here, like pronto. They've killed David and have tried to kill me as well. These people are vicious. Let's get moving."

"I'm packing a bag. It'll only take me a few more minutes."

She headed back to a small bedroom and we followed. I asked, "So tell us how this got started. David said you were involved with some computer geek?"

She had a suitcase open on the bed and had been throwing clothes and a few other personal items in it. She opened a drawer and added to the pile. "Yes. I clean houses to make extra money. I started working for Lincoln a few months back. He's a nice enough guy and, well, you know, one thing led to another and we ended up in bed. He likes to get high after sex and one night after a few joints he starts bragging about this thing he was involved in."

"The Exodus Project," Samantha said.

"That's right. Starts telling me they wouldn't have a chance of pulling it off without him and that when the shit goes down, it would be worldwide news. And all because he figured out how to make it happen. Said the Christians in this country would, and I quote, "Want revenge on every Muslim on the planet."

She finished packing and closed the suitcase. She said, "That's all I know. But the look in his eyes scared me. So I decided I needed to tell someone. My mother loves reading David's columns and since he's an investigative reporter, I contacted him."

She teared up. "You said they killed him. How exactly?" she asked.

Samantha looked at me and I gave a slight nod. She gave Rebecca a brief account of what happened at David's house and in the cemetery, while glossing over some of the gorier parts.

I lifted the suitcase. "Come on, ladies, let's skedaddle. It's after ten o'clock and time's a wastin'."

We made it outside the cottage into the unseasonably warm fall night, but stopped when we heard a sound. It was a car and it was headed up the driveway.

Chapter Eleven

There was no way we'd be able to get into my car and past the one coming up the driveway. I asked Rebecca which way to the mansion from here and she pointed off to the left of the cottage to a path that disappeared into the woods. We ran in that direction and had just made it into the darkness under low-hanging branches when a Cadillac Escalade pulled up behind my car, blocking it.

I stopped Samantha and Rebecca a short ways down the path and the three of us watched from behind a large oak tree as J.B. and another guy got out of the Cadillac. I could see Winston behind the wheel, holding an ice pack up to his jaw.

Both men moved forward with guns out as they checked my car and moved to the door of the cottage. I held my own down at my side, the safety off.

Samantha asked, "He has to be working for Deveraux if they're already here."

I thought if that was true, how were they already at Phoenix Hill Tavern when we took off from David's house. They weren't looking for us in the cemetery, trying to cut us off. They were inside the tavern. Hell, Winston wasn't even looking towards David's house. Then it hit me. They weren't tracking Samantha, they were tracking me. They must have put a GPS device somewhere on my car. I swore under my breath. I should have thought of a tracker when they showed up at Phoenix Hill, and I didn't. I was slipping and it could get us killed.

J.B. stayed outside while the hired goon checked the house. It didn't take long. He came back out and said something to J.B. who then looked around at the surrounding woods. He then said something to Winston who headed back down the drive, probably to the mansion.

J.B. started turning around in a slow circle and shouted into the darkness surrounding him, "Alright, Vic. I know you're out there somewhere. You win. I won't hold the taser to the family jewels against you. Heck, if I'd been in your position, I might have done the same thing. You and I can work something out on the girl. That fifty-fifty deal you made me would work. But this is a onetime offer, Vic. My boys and I are getting a little tired of putting up with your shit."

Samantha grabbed me by the arm and whispered, "You know him?" I could hear the hurt in her voice, could feel the way her nails dug into my bomber jacket.

At that moment I was really glad she left her sword in the car. It was near pitch black under the oak tree, but I didn't have to see her eyes to feel the look she was giving me.

"Look, it's complicated. When we get out of this, I'll explain. I'm not giving you up. You have my word on that."

She said, "You're pathetic. Like your word is worth anything. I really thought you were on my side." Feeling betrayed, she let go of my arm with a shove and moved away a few feet from me. The rebuke in the move cut me to the quick, though I didn't blame her. The tactical advantage the space gave her as a black belt wasn't lost on me either. At the moment, though, I had bigger problems.

Rebecca remained silent, but I could only imagine what she was thinking. I whispered to her, "We need to hide out somewhere. Where can we can go to besides the mansion?"

"There's an old barn a couple of fields over. I've walked there many times. I think I can get us there in the dark."

J.B. yelled out, "Tick-tock-tick-tock, Vic."

I told Rebecca to lead the way and whispered for Samantha to follow her. She hesitated for a moment, but then started off and I fell in behind her. At one point there was a break in the trees and we could pick our way by the moonlight. I watched as Samantha slipped off her heels, and enjoyed the sway of her hips as she picked up the pace to catch up to Rebecca.

We hadn't gone very far when we heard yet someone else coming up the driveway. We were still close enough to see through the mesh of leaves as a van pulled up and parked behind the Caddy. The four men we had seen outside David's house, still dressed in coveralls, got out, each one holding some sort of small machine gun.

J.B. asked, "Who the hell are you guys?" He and his hired help still had their guns in their hands, but held them out to the side.

The driver of the van asked, "Where's the girl?"

"What girl?" J.B. decided to play dumb. Turned out to be a bad move. The driver shot J.B.'s henchman with a short burst from the machine gun, the bullets causing him to dance backwards a few steps, and then he went down hard, collapsing into the shrubs.

The gunman leveled his gun at J.B. and said, "Let me ask this one more time, where's the girl?" This time J.B. didn't hesitate.

"We followed her here, but she wasn't inside. She has to be here someplace. We think she's with a bounty hunter named Victor McCain. That's his car. I know him. He's a real pain in the ass, but good at what he does, a professional. Let me find them for you. I can talk to Vic and get him to hand over the girl and save you a lot of trouble."

The driver considered this for a moment, then asked "What about the other girl?"

"What other girl? Who the hell you talking about, man? Don't shoot me, man, I don't have a clue who you're talking about."

The driver motioned for two of the other guys to search the house. I didn't need to hear any more and motioned Rebecca to keep going.

Samantha said, her voice low, "You lying son of a bitch. I trusted you."

"And you still can," I shot back. "Give me a chance to explain when there is less of a chance of getting our asses shot off, will you?"

She gave it a rest as we followed Rebecca off the path, and moving as quietly as we could, to the barn. We were about ten minutes into our walk when we once again heard the short bark of a machine gun. Looks like they didn't feel they needed J.B anymore. I felt myself grow angry. J.B. was a good guy and didn't deserve to be shot like some rabid dog. There was going to be hell to pay when this was finished. Literally. Samantha wasn't the only one who now wanted retribution.

It wasn't long before we could see flashlights back on the path headed towards the mansion. It wouldn't take them long to figure we weren't there either and for them to broaden their search. I had to wonder what Winston was doing right at this moment. If he had any sense, he would have bolted at the first sounds of automatic gunfire. Three flashlights meant they most likely left one guy back with the cars, so circling back there would be risky.

The barn looked several decades old, with planks missing here and there, and smelled of hay. The front doors were open so we went inside. I took out my iPhone and from the phone's soft glow, I could see the barn was filled mostly with square bales of hay. Nowadays most people used round bale, so this was something of a surprise.

I walked over to a missing slat and watched the trail leading back to the cottage. I couldn't see anyone. Samantha rounded on me and asked, "Who hired you? Deveraux had no clue who you were, neither did Kevin, so it wasn't them. So who hired you? My father?"

I told Rebecca to keep an eye out while I searched the barn. "No. It wasn't your father. It was someone above his pay grade." I felt my jaw clenching in irritation and forced myself to relax. It wasn't her fault I was in this mess. Her only confidant had been murdered, her father had sent a minion from Hell to find her and then she finds out I wasn't what I claimed I was.

"Oh come off it, Vic. No one's above my father when it comes to the Church. Deveraux offered you a million. How much did you sell me out for, Vic? Or is that even your real name?"

I found empty canning jars on a work bench near the front door, as well as an old red five gallon container sitting on top of a broken down lawnmower. I unscrewed the cap and took a sniff. Gasoline. I looked around and found a dusty blanket on the ground and brought it with the can over to the bench, shaking the dirt out of the blanket.

"Unlike you, Vic is my real name. I told you, my situation is complicated. And you're wrong. There is someone above your father."

I don't know why I felt the need to explain to her and get her to understand. One thing I've learned as a bounty hunter is not to get attached to who you had caught. Everyone has a sad story. Some would beg, some would even plead for you to let them go. Some offered money, or drugs, or sex. Keeping a distance between you and the perp made things easier. Point is, I had her in my custody and if I did get her out of here safely, I was planning on turning her over to Satan, so best to keep my distance.

Or was I going to turn her over? The more the night went on, I became less sure of exactly what I was going to do with her. Would trading her for my brother's soul be the right thing to do? In the abstract, from my point of view, yes it was. I trade her for my brother. If she believed in God, with any luck, He would protect her, at least in the afterlife, if not this one. My brother was screwed if I didn't bring her in. There was only one person in the world that could save my brother, and I was it. Yet deep down inside, I felt a need for her to understand why I was doing what I was doing.

"Oh, give me a break. I had a reason for changing my name and you know it. How complicated could it be for you, Vic? You've seen what these people are like. You're in bed with them so how are you any different?"

I used the glow of my phone to see by, as I ripped the blanket into thin strips. I didn't reply to her, concentrating on what I was doing. Samantha walked to me and leaning back on the bench said, "Damn it Vic, answer me." When I said nothing, she continued, "Tell me this, at least. How much did it take to buy you?"

For several seconds I didn't reply. I laid the blanket strips onto the bench, and then held onto the edge of the bench myself as I bowed my head. "My brother's soul."

I could hear Samantha's sharp intake of breath. I couldn't look at her or Rebecca. "The Devil came to me and told me if I found you and brought you to him, that he would release my brother from a soul contract he signed."

She crossed her arms across her chest. "Right. You expect me to believe that you had a face to face with the Devil? Do I *look* like an idiot?"

I felt very tired. I went back to my work, unscrewing the gas cap and filling two jars with gasoline. I soaked two blanket strips in gasoline as well and then dropped one end of the strips into the jars and put the screw lids back on top, making two quick Molotov cocktails.

"So asks the woman who earlier this evening told me about vampires. Look, at this point, whether you believe me or not, doesn't really matter. But your dad prays to him. Eamon was back on Earth because of him, and I've met the prick. And if I really was anxious to hand you over, I've had several chances to do so and haven't. You should be asking yourself why not?"

She furrowed her brow and I could tell she was doing just that: thinking about why I hadn't turned her over to Deveraux. I took a couple of the hay bales, ripped them apart and spread them across the barn's dirt floor. Then I poured the rest of the gasoline onto the hay.

Looking alarmed, Rebecca asked, "What the hell are you doing?"

"Backup plan. Always have a backup plan. Tell us everything you told David about the Exodus Project?"

"I told you most of it. Lincoln was bragging that he had solved some big technical problem they were having with the computers and the computer virus. He told me about how they were going to hit Christian schools and start a religious war with Muslims.

"I was with him again last night. He left his computer laptop on while he went to take a shower. I checked his computer and it had some file up and I took a picture of the documents he had open. They were all technical mumbo-jumbo to me. So I took pictures of them with my phone and then texted them to David."

"Do you still have them on your phone?"

She nodded yes. "Send them to me."

Pointing to Samantha, she asked, "Why? If you were hired to find her, why do you care?"

"Just do it, please." I shoved my hands in my pockets, suddenly exhausted. "I'll say it again, it's complicated. If you two don't want my help, fine by me. But if you do, you need to start letting me help you."

I gave her my cell number and I took her place watching for the bad guys while she texted the photos to me.

Samantha walked up beside me and stood there looking out into the night for a bit, content to listen to the night sounds before she said anything. I could tell she was thinking hard as she began biting her bottom lip again.

"You said I should be asking myself why you didn't turn me over to Deveraux. Well, I have and I can't come up with anything. Rebecca's right, why even help me at all?"

I said nothing.

"I mean, if you really did promise Satan you'd find me for him, why didn't you just hand me over right away when you had the chance?"

I said nothing. My phone beeped as the photos from Rebecca found their way to my account.

She laid a hand on my arm, gently this time. "Talk to me, Vic. I'm just trying to understand what's going on."

"I'll tell you later."

She reached up and took my chin in her hand, turning my face towards her. I could see her eyes in the starlight falling through the gap in the barn wall, eyes mixed with fear and concern. "Why won't you tell me now?"

I pointed off into the darkness. "Because they're coming."

Chapter Twelve

The flashlights were headed in our direction. Guess someone at the mansion had told them about the barn.

Frightened, Rebecca asked, "Why don't we make a run for it?"

"We won't get very far. I have a flashlight app on my phone, but we can only move so fast and Samantha isn't exactly wearing hiking boots." She did look damn good though, in her black evening dress with her coat unzipped, her feet bare. I gave myself a mental slap to get back to business.

"They have better flashlights and are better equipped. I think it's time to even the odds some." I looked at Samantha. "Just a wild guess, you're using a throw away cell phone, right?

"Yes, why?" She got her phone out of her coat pocket.

"Anyone else have that number besides David?" There wasn't much time before the bad guys made their appearance.

"No. He got the phone for me. I only used it to call him and vice versa."

"Good, then you won't miss it. Give your number to Rebecca so she can call you on it right now. I'd use David's phone, but it doesn't have a speakerphone option."

She did so and Rebecca, nervous and fumble-fingered, took two attempts to dial the number. I took the phone and pressed the speakerphone button, went over to the stacked bales of hay, pulled one out and placed the phone down behind it.

Then I walked over and picked up the two Molotov cocktails. "Leave the connection open. I want the two of you to go a little ways into the woods, but stay where you can still see the light from my phone. When I flash you twice, here's what I want you to do."

I told them and then led them out to the edge of the woods. "If you two bolt on me, all three of us are as good as dead. Or at least Rebecca and I are." I looked at Samantha. "You'll get to live, at least for a little while. Until they get their money back, at any rate. And before they do that, I'll come back and haunt you from beyond the grave."

Samantha asked, "How do I know I can trust you, Vic?" She looked me straight in the eyes. No sarcasm, no anger. Just a simple question.

"You don't. But believe me when I say, right now, the only thing between you and a date with the Devil: is me."

I smiled and said, "But if they kill me, feel free to run like hell." I turned and walked back to the barn. There was an old tractor parked next to it on the side closest to the woods, and I kneeled down behind it. I looked through some missing slats to the other side and could see the coverall crew was almost to the barn. I sheltered my iPhone in my bomber jacket and turned on the flashlight app, which uses the phone's camera flash as a bright flashlight. I stuck my hand through the gap in the barn wall and showed the light around the inside of the barn briefly, then turned the app off.

Just as I hoped, the three men who were approaching saw the light and broke into a quick jog towards the barn. I waited a moment and faced my phone in the direction of the women and clicked my phone on and off twice, with the more gentle glow of the startup screen facing towards them.

From inside the barn I heard Rebecca say, "Here they come, hide!" Followed by Samantha saying, "Be quiet or you'll give us away."

The men approached the front of the barn and two men came in as one of them shouted, "We know you're in here. Come out now and we won't hurt you. You have our word."

The other one said, "Do you smell that? Smells like gasoline."

"We're coming out," shouted Samantha. "Please don't shoot!"

The men moved a little further into the barn and that was enough for me. I took my Bic lighter out of my pocket, struck it and set the blanket strip on fire and tossed the Molotov cocktail through the gap in the slats, hitting the ancient lawnmower on the front grill, shattering the glass.

The gasoline ignited in a ball of fire and the small explosion set the gasoline soaked hay into an instant blaze. The old barn went up instantly in flames. The men screamed as they were engulfed by the fire. I lit the other Molotov cocktail and threw it between them and the door.

The men ran from the barn with their clothing on fire. They dropped their guns as they fell on the ground, rolling, in an attempt to put out the flames that engulfed them. Two down, one more to go. I pulled out my own gun and turned the corner of the barn, searching for the third man.

From behind me, I heard, "Drop the weapon and turn around." Looks like he found me. He must have run to the back of the barn and circled behind me when the fire started.

I did as he asked. I dropped my gun and turned around slowly to find myself looking down the short barrel of his machine gun. I wish I could say my life flashed before my eyes, but it didn't. The one thought that went through my mind was…figures. I can't tell you how many nights I lay in my bunk in Afghanistan wondering if I would die the next day and how. Would I get taken out by an IED, or would a sniper get me? I envisioned a million different ways to die.

After I got home from the war, I had dreams about how I'd be busting down some door and a perp or his girlfriend would shoot me. But I never dreamed this would be the way I'd go out. As I said: figures.

"Hey, did you bring any marshmallows? Or maybe hot dogs?" I asked. "As long as we have this fire going, we might as well take advantage of it." I sniffed the air as the smell of burning flesh was carried on the otherwise pleasant night breeze. "Smells like crispy critters. Guess two rats went up with the fire."

I gave him my best what the hell grin. He wasn't impressed. "You must be the bounty hunter. For what you did to Frank and Willy, I should make you suffer like they did. But tell me where the women are and I'll kill you quickly. You're a dead man either way. But how you die is up to you."

Like hell he would. I knew telling him I didn't know wasn't a good answer, as it hadn't done much for J.B.'s sidekick. I also knew I couldn't tell him where the girls were either. Before I could come up with another snide remark, a man stepped out from behind the tractor, put the muzzle of his gun against the back of the man's head and said, "I will give you one chance to lower your gun or I will blow your head off." Politely said, but with an unmistaken authority.

The gunman looked to be Latino. He was of average height, but broad in the shoulders, somewhere north of thirty years old, wearing a dark jacket, washed out jeans and worn leather boots. His hair was cropped very close to his skull and in the flickering light from the fire, I couldn't help but notice the tattoos that ran down his neck and beneath the collar of his shirt. Gang tattoos. Mexican gang tattoos.

The gun hand was steady and never wavered. The barn fire was picking up steam and the heat was growing intense, along with the situation.

The man holding his gun on me dropped his weapon. My savior took him by the collar of his coveralls and, keeping the gun pressed to his head, led him away from the now raging inferno and towards the woods. He nodded for me to follow. When I bent down to pick up my gun he said, "Take it easy my friend, use only the fingers and grab by the barrel."

Since he was the man with the plan, I did as he said. His accent was definitely from south of the border, but his English was better than some Kentuckians. He moved with an easy grace, like one of the pros on Dancing with the Stars. Once we were by the woods, he forced the man in coveralls to his knees, looked at me and said, "Throw the gun."

I did so. And I did so slowly. He watched me carefully, like a panther watching a rabbit he has trapped between his paws.

"Señoritas, please join us." He waited a moment. "I know you are here, I watched you walking in the trees. I will not hurt you, I promise."

After a moment Samantha and Rebecca came out from hiding, Rebecca still holding her suitcase. They approached to within a few feet, but no closer. They looked at me and then back to the man holding the gun. Neither came to stand by me. Probably a smart move on their part.

"So you are Victor McCain, the bounty hunter?" he asked me, while never taking his gun from Deveraux's man.

"That's right. But call me Vic. All my friends do, especially those holding a gun."

"A bounty hunter who looks for women?"

Not a man into witty banter. "Just one of them, the mouthy redhead. Her name's Samantha. We came out to try and save the other one from the Church of the Light Reclaimed. Her name's Rebecca."

He looked at Samantha. "So, this man was looking for you, but you come to help this other señorita?"

Ever have one of those moments, when you know you're whole life may depend on the answer, but you have no clue why? This seemed to be that kind of moment. The man's attitude remained casual, but there seemed to be more to what he was asking than simple curiosity. It was as if my life depended on her answer.

Samantha looked at me for what seemed a long time. "Yeah," she said. "We came here together. He saved my life earlier tonight. He also tried to help save the life of a friend of mine, though he died anyway, but it wasn't Victor's fault. And he was doing what he could to save us again when you showed up."

Samantha didn't mention that I deceived her from the beginning and that she wasn't aware I was a bounty hunter until *after* J.B. arrived. And that I was doing as much to save my ass as I was theirs when he showed up. This conversation took place while the barn fire roared, baking the side of my face.

"Who's your jefe, Victor McCain? Who do you work for?" the man asked.

Once again, I knew the answer was important, without really knowing why. I also knew lying to this man, whoever he was, would be a really bad move.

"I was hired by Satan, to track down Miranda Chernenko, who, it turns out, is really Samantha Tyler."

He pursed his lips and nodded. If he thought I was nuts for saying I'd been hired by Satan, he kept it to himself. "And, you do this willingly?"

"No," I said. "I took the job because my brother sold his soul to the Devil and I was told if I found her and took her to him, he would tear up the soul contract and release his soul back to him."

"Tough deal, ah?" the man said. "So, Victor, why help the woman? Your job was to turn her in to the Dark One." Both Samantha and Rebecca had asked me the same question and I hadn't answered them. Mainly because I wasn't sure what the answer would be. I knew this man would not settle for an 'I'll tell you later.'

"I've been looking for a different way out. One that would save my brother, but not require me to hand her over."

"And you find the way?" Samantha watched me intently, as I considered my answer.

I sighed. "No. I haven't. I'm still working on it."

The man in coveralls, kneeling in the soft grass of the field, said, "Don't kill me, please don't kill me."

The man pushed forward with the barrel of the gun against the kneeling man's head and said, "Shhhh. Your final day is coming amigo, but now we are discussing Victor. Take your time to pray to God and the Saints so they may forgive your sins."

He continued, "If you don't find a better way, would you still save your brother instead of her?"

I could easily say no, that I'd changed my mind, that I would never do such a thing now. But I knew that was a lie. And while I never had a problem lying to people to get the information I wanted, I told him the truth. "I don't know. I'm still working on that one, too."

I thought this would anger the man, and that I would find myself kneeling in the mud, asking for him not to punch my ticket. But life is full of surprises. "I like your answer, Victor. I respect an honest man in situations like this."

"You keep using my name, but I don't know yours."

He smiled, revealing several teeth capped in gold. "My name is Dominic Montoya."

"Jesus," Samantha said, "It's the Hand of God."

Chapter Thirteen

So God's trigger man on Earth is a tattooed Mexican cartel gang banger. You might as well have told me my great Uncle Rupert, the one that hates kids and loves his Irish Whiskey, is really Santa Claus. I could see the shock on Samantha's face, and the awe on Rebecca's face. Guess the man had a reputation.

Samantha said, "You were supposed to meet me at the Down and Dirty tonight, but you never showed." Her tone made her statement an accusation. To a man holding a gun, no less. Tough girl.

"I was busy with another thing. I got there late but you were gone fast. I heard the men in the Cadillac talking about you and Victor. They say they had a tracker on Victor's auto and when they follow for you, I follow them. I was curious why they want you bad. Then I was in the parking lot at Phoenix Hill when you left the cementerio. Victor, very nice plan. Very nice."

I shook my head. "Not really. I sucker punched him. Not one of my proudest moments."

He shrugged his shoulders. "We do what we has to do" He continued, "When the men left to follow for you, I did the same and lucky you, it seems. Which brings us to this man," he said, gesturing with his free hand to the man kneeling before him. "I know he kill two men this evening" He pushed the man's head lightly with his gun. "What is your name?"

The man's crying had stopped. He said in a very soft voice, "Dutch. Dutch Simpson."

"Who is your jefe?" Montoya's words were simply said, but they carried an undertone of authority.

"I work for Preston Deveraux. He works for the Church of the Light Reclaimed."

"And what were your instructions for tonight?"

"Go fuck yourself. Let's get this over with."

"As you wish." The Hand of God motioned for the two women to turn around. Rebecca did so and hid her face in trembling hands. Samantha continued to watch Montoya, her face showing no emotion, as he prepared to execute the man before him. I guessed she wanted to see some payback for what happened to David. But I couldn't believe what I was seeing.

"Wait," I said, "You don't have to do this. Why don't we just turn him over to the

cops. That's what our legal system is for. Let them take care of this douche bag."

"Sorry, but I deliver an Old Testament justice. I answer to no earthly jurisdiction."

And with that he pulled the trigger. Simpson toppled face first into the short green grass of the pasture, while some of his blood and brains sprayed onto my boots. I felt anger at his death. I have no problem killing people when there is no other choice. Hell, I'd just killed two men by burning them to death and shot another man to death earlier in the evening. But I killed them because that was my only option if I wanted to keep breathing. Montoya did have a choice and there were other options besides blowing the man's head off. Simpson may have been evil, but he was defenseless and no threat to us. We could have tied him up and hauled his ass off to the cops.

And now I had to wonder if I was next. I found out soon enough as The Hand of God focused his attention back on me.

Montoya said, "Step out from the gun and go with the women."

I released the breath I'd been holding and did as he asked and stood by Samantha. He picked up my gun, slid out the clip and ejected the round I had hot in the chamber. He put the extra round back in the magazine and then tossed me my gun and clip. "For now, put the clip in your coat pocket and the gun back in its holster. If I see you looking for them without my permit, I will kill you."

Of this I had no doubts. "Should I say thank you, or what?"

"You should say thank you, God" He looked at the barn fire and said, "Vamonos. Soon someone will see the flames and call it in. We go before authorities arrive."

The man had a point and we started back to the cottage at a brisk walk, leaving the raging fire behind. Considering the amount of dead bodies, it would pay to be anywhere but here when the cops arrived.

Montoya asked, "What was your deal with el Diablo? Tell me

specifically what you promised to do and when."

I told him the arrangements Satan and I had made. "Then there is time to decide what you do. When Luci makes a deal, he must adhere to the agreement, down to the last letter. You have put your own soul at risk by agree to work for Luci. If you do this thing, then your soul will also be lost. Your brother cannot be saved. Once he agree to sell his soul he was lost to you and to God."

"I thought God allowed anyone to ask forgiveness for his sins and to enter Heaven if he or she truly means it. And why do you call him Luci?"

He smiled. "Luci is what I call the evil one as I will not honor him with any other name. As for forgiveness, your brother made a deal with the devil, Victor. Even if you deliver Samantha to Luci and he tears up your brother's soul contract, your brother will still go to Hell. Luci will find a way to trick you or him. You must accept this fact. God gives us the freedom to choose our path in life and death and your brother has chosen the path to Hell. He knew this when he sold his soul."

To hell with that, I thought. There had to be a way to save my brother and I would find it. I kept this to myself, however, as I had no desire to join Simpson in the great beyond. As we neared the cottage, I said to Montoya, "There was a fourth man. They must have left him waiting at the cottage."

Montoya said, "He is not a problem."

"What, you killed him, too?"

In the pale moon's light, I could see Montoya's jaw muscles clench. "I do not answer you, comprende? Thank you God put me here to save you tonight like the women. I do what I do on God's behalf, not yours or another's."

"What ever happened to turn the other cheek? Love thy neighbor? Do unto others as you would have them do unto you?" I could feel myself growing more angry and I wasn't sure why. My frustration level was shooting through the roof and I was having a real problem putting a lid on my emotions.

There could be little doubt things were spinning out of my control. With the Hand of God on the scene, I didn't know what this would mean for my brother. A new dynamic had been introduced and I would have to find a way to adapt. Making decisions when you are anything other than level-headed is a short path to disaster.

When we reached the cottage, Montoya asked the women to wait by the door as he motioned me to follow him to the back of the van. He opened the door and inside there were six bodies. David's body was there as well as that of the two Ice Pick Lovers, Kevin, J.B., and his hired hand. Guess the Church didn't suffer failure when it comes to their assassins. "God's love means nothing to men who would do something like this. Do you recognize any of these unfortunates?" he asked.

I told him who each corpse was and then told him how David died. He crossed himself and said a short prayer for the dead. Montoya said, "I sad that the reporter is dead. He was a very, very good man. He was the one that contact me first, through an intermediary, and asked me to meet with Miss Tyler."

"So what now?" I asked. This simple question could very well decide not only my brother's fate, but mine.

"What are you going to do with Rebecca? She cannot stay here," Montoya said.

"I have no real plans other than to get her away from here and someplace the Church won't find her."

"Very well, I know a place I can take her where she be safe, for now at least." We closed the doors on the back of the van.

"And Samantha?" I asked.

"That will be up to her." He motioned for me to return to the women, who were speaking in low tones as we approached. Montoya said to them, "Here is the plan. Rebecca, I will take you away from the guys that are looking for you. Don't you have a car here, eh?"

"No," she said, "I was going to ride with Victor and Samantha."

"You can go with me. My car is just down the street. And you, Samantha, who would you like to go with?"

I was surprised at the question, assuming she would ride with the Hand of God. She said, "I'll ride with Vic. Someone has to keep him out of trouble." She took a few steps until she was standing close to me and I felt a surge run through my body as if an electrical charge had jumped from her body to mine. I don't know why she was staying with me, but I didn't care.

"OK. You two follow me. After I see to it that Rebecca is good, the three of us will find a place to speak."

I jabbed my thumb at the van. "What should we do about this?"

"There is no time. Someone will find them soon enough. The

Lord's will be done."

I said to Rebecca, "Call your sister and tell her not to come anywhere near this place."

"I will." She gave Samantha and me quick hugs. "Thank you. I'd be dead if it wasn't for the two of you." We said our goodbyes and she and Montoya quickly headed down the drive.

Before Samantha and I got in the Chevelle, I ran my hand under the edge of the car and found the GPS device, a Spark Nano, stuck to the underside of the back bumper. I shook my head again and said, "I should have guessed this right off." I turned it off and put it in my jacket pocket.

We got in the car and I did a quick turn around and scooted by the van with its cargo of the dead. Won't the cops be happy when they find this little dust up? She asked me what was in the back of the van and I told her. Then I said, "I'm more than a little surprised that you would get back in the car with me, you know, considering."

"I have faith in you, Vic. From what I've seen tonight, I don't think you're the kind of guy that would just hand me over like that. Besides, I have way too many sins of my own to go car hopping with the Hand of God." She let out a small laugh, but then turned more serious. "Let's just do our best to convince him to do something about the Exodus Project."

I found it ironic that a woman like Samantha, who believed God was dead was talking about faith, and more to the point, faith in me. She knew how important she was to me when it came to saving my brother's soul and knew I still had not decided on if I would make the trade.

Yet here she was, slouched in her seat, feet up on the dashboard, riding into the night with me. While she looked exhausted from the evening's events, she, at the same time, looked more relaxed. Perhaps having the Hand of God on the scene gave her more hope. It had done just the opposite for me. His pronouncement that there was no way to save my brother's soul had me worried.

We soon caught up to Montoya and Thomas as they were getting into a green Jeep Wrangler. He pulled out and we fell in behind him. We hit Covered Bridge Road and headed back towards the city. It wasn't long before a fire truck and two police cars raced past us going in the direction of the farm. The shit was getting ready to hit the fan and I, for one, felt happy I wouldn't be there when it did.

Chapter Fourteen

We made our way back into the city. Montoya pulled into a gas station on Market Street. We pulled up next to him and the zip flap on his window was down. He said, "Wait here. I'll be back in about fifteen minutes."

Rebecca gave us a shy wave and with that, he pulled back out and was gone. I slid my phone out of my pocket and said, "Let's see what documents Rebecca sent me." I thumbed over to my text messages and downloaded the images. I leaned to the middle of the car so that Samantha could look as well. Once again I caught the hint of her perfume, this time mixed with a whiff of smoke from the barn fire.

I swallowed hard and briefly closed my eyes, resisting the urge to move even closer to her. I'd been hired to find this woman and had done so. But here I was wanting to take her into my arms, and world be damned when it came to the consequences. My body was having a fight with my brain and my brain was starting to lose the fight. And if that happened, I might just lose both my soul and that of my brother's.

I had to wonder if she was feeling the same thing, as she was leaning in closer than she needed in order to view my phone screen. I had to snap out of it! I was starting to think like a love-sick high school kid.

Lucky for me, the pictures finished their download. The first few images were a little blurry, but appeared to be some parts order list. It looked to be all computer equipment type-stuff and in large quantities: motherboards, computer cases, and the like, with five hundred of each. So they were going to build five hundred machines? And then what?

The last two images were of a flier. It was for an academic tournament to be held on December 20th called *God's Vision Academic Challenge*. Parochial schools from around the region would be competing on the same day using something called God's Vision 2012 software to compete and earn prizes for the schools. The second page touted the fact that the software and the computers would be donated by some outfit called Inspiration Global Software. Guess we now knew where the five hundred computers were going to end up.

"Have you ever heard of Inspiration Global Software?" I asked. She shook her head no. I switched over to the browser on my phone and Googled the company. There was a place holder website listing their address in St. Matthews, an eastern suburb of Louisville. They had a phone number as well, but when I called I got a recording asking me to call back during business hours.

The only other information on the site said they were a company that designed educational software for parochial schools and that more information would be available soon. There was one link, and that was to a page that listed the same information as the flier.

If they were planning a computer attack, this appeared to be how they would go about it. Donate the computers with the computer virus built into the software. And they were going to use this to start a religious war? How the hell they planned on doing that was anybody's guess. I'd known some people to get really ticked off over a computer virus, but mad enough to start a war? Maybe enough to slug a geek, but not enough to go to war.

Montoya pulled back up next to us, Rebecca no longer in the car. He offered up no explanation as to where he'd taken her and we didn't ask. He suggested we hit the Dizzy Whizz burger joint, which was fine with me. I'd spent my last meal in Louisville there before shipping off for basic training at Fort Leonard Wood, Missouri by catching a Greyhound Bus a few blocks over. Besides, nothing like a little grease after offing a few guys.

We followed him over to the diner and I thought about the evening on the drive over. No matter what happened before my 6 P.M. deadline, life forever changed with my killing of three men and one former man. My fingerprints were going to show up at two crime scenes. And since my prints were on file with the state as part of the licensing process to become a bounty hunter, they would be looking for me—sooner rather than later.

I dialed my brother's number again, but it went straight to voicemail. Samantha asked, "Are you and your brother close?"

"Not overly. But he and my mother are. And if he died, my mom would be crushed. If she ever found out he sold his soul, I can't imagine what it would do to her."

"How about your dad? Is he still in the picture?"

"Nah. He died of a heart attack. Worked his ass off to save enough money to put us through college, but Mikey flunked out and I ended up leaving right after I graduated from college to join the Army to kick some Al Qaeda backside."

We pulled in at the Dizzy Whizz next to Montoya and the three of us went inside. After ordering, we took a table near the back. We had to make quite the scene. Between my size, Montoya's gang tats and the beauty of Samantha, we were a strange mix. She brought her case inside with her and sat next to me. Perhaps she planned on using it to cut her burger in half. She did a good enough job on Eamon. I doubted a knock down drag out would take place at the Dizzy Whizz, but guess it's better to be prepared than not.

Sitting this close to Samantha was messing with my thought process. There had to be a pheromone reaction going on between us, at least on my end.

Dominic Montoya broke my reverie and asked, "So, now that you and me get to have our sit down Miss Tyler, what I can do for you?"

Samantha gave him the quick rundown on what she knew about what the Church had in motion with the Exodus Project and her stealing the thirty million dollars to slow them down. I added my input on the documents that Rebecca had texted to me. We also told him about what happened at David's house and Deveraux's part in our little drama. Montoya chomped down on a couple of fries while he listened to us without interrupting.

"This weekend is critical for the Church. I overheard my father say they would shell out millions for something that's going to take place here in Louisville. It's why I took off from Philadelphia a couple weeks ago with the money and came here. David and I were trying to figure out what. Now you know what we know."

When we finished he said, "I do not see what I can do for you. This is not the type of thing I get into it. And like you, I do not see how the Satanists plan on causing a religious war with a computer virus. If they plan a physical attack on children, it will be more different. But with what you tell me tonight, I do not think I can be of service to you."

Samantha leaned forward and said, "It has to be something big, though. There have been messages going back and forth between my father and people involved. They've been really jazzed over this thing. Plus, I know for a fact they have a lot of money wrapped up in this attack. You have to help us." There was desperation in her voice and exasperation on her face.

Montoya was unperturbed. He took a bite of his burger and said around the mouthful, "Keep digging, I will give you the number to my cell. It is only good this weekend. If you come up with something, then call me. I am in town one, maybe two days. Without more information, I cannot help you as I am here on other business. If I hear something, I will be in touch."

"So, what, that's it? You're just blowing us off?" She threw her hands up in the air. "I don't believe this. David lost his life over this," she said. "The Church is going to great lengths to silence anyone who knows anything at all about the Exodus Project. There has to be something you can do?"

"I did. I save your lives. I know you are upset. But I get ask to help in many things and many ways, and I only have so much time to give. Believe me, my friend, when I tell you there are problems more dangerous than computer virus. As I say, find me more on the threat and I will consider lending more aid. Until then, I cannot."

I said, "What about Deveraux? You know he's responsible for several murders. Aren't you going to dole out some Old Testament justice to him like you did Simpson?"

"At some point, I may have to deal with Deveraux the same way I did Simpson, but that is not my focus. If I kill everyone who committed murder in this world, I never sleep. As I say, I have something much more important that I work on. Give me more and then we see."

I was really ticked. I had a timeline to save my brother and, coincidentally, the Church was running on the same timeline. I don't like coincidences. It frustrated me to have a resource like the Hand of God in town, and for him not to help at such a critical point just blows. With his help, I could perhaps save my brother and protect Samantha. But, without him? It seemed an impossible task. What if my handing over Samantha brought about the holy war the Church had planned? The pressure to figure out this Rubik cube of a problem was mounting.

Montoya said, "One more question, Victor. Why you?"

My blood pressure shot up and I could feel my face flush red at the question. "Perhaps it's because I'm damn good at what I do. Did you stop to think about that? Samantha slid a hand over top of mine and gave it a squeeze.

He said, "Please forgive me, but you do not understand me. I'm not suggesting you are not good at your job. But if Luci had Miss Tyler's address, why involve you at all? Why not have members of the Church go to her address? Luci is a creature as old as Heaven itself. If he chose you, he did so for more reasons than the obvious. It is something you have to think about."

I cooled off as I realized he was right. I took a moment, considering what he said. "It could be as simple as he knew I would do what it takes to help my brother."

"Maybe," he said.

He ate the rest of his burger and fries and then asked Samantha, "You now have a choice to make before I go. If you want, you can go with me, and I do for you as I do for Miss Thomas. I will see to it you are a safe from harm, at least for now. There will be nothing Victor can do about it. Or I can keep him here until you find your own way from this diner. Or you can continue to work with the bounty hunter. The choice is yours."

His hand was resting in his coat pocket, the same one where he stashed his gun. I kept my hands resting on the table top, in plain sight, and concentrated on not making any sudden movements.

"That's O.K. I know a big part of the Exodus Project happens this weekend, and if I'm in hiding, I won't be able to help stop it. And if you won't step up and do something about it, then I guess that leaves me." She looked at me. "I don't think Victor has it in him to turn me over to Satan. At least he's offered to help me and I plan on holding him to that commitment."

"How can you be so sure about a man you just met?" asked the Hand of God.

She gave a dazzling, but weary smile and said, "I have faith Mr. Montoya. I have faith. Maybe not in God, but I do in Victor. And I have a big shiny sword."

Honestly, I thought she was nuts. Lord knows I didn't have faith I wouldn't turn her over in exchange for my brother. In fact, I was rather conflicted about the whole thing. Blood is thicker than most anything else and I was on a mission to find a way to save Mikey. What if turning over Samantha was my only option to save him? I still had no clue what I would do. If I was in her shoes, I would want to run as far away from me as possible.

Montoya said, "The choice is yours, my friend. But let me say this to you, Victor. If you hand over Miss Tyler to Luci, I will make it a point to hunt you down myself. Comprende? You have my word."

I would normally have had any one of a dozen smart ass replies, like I always do when someone threatens me. Not this time. Not with this man. I said, "If I do that, then the Hand of God won't have to hunt me down, you'll find me in my office waiting."

He took out a pen and, on a napkin, wrote down his cell number and passed it over to me. "So be it. Good luck to you and may God protect you." And with that The Hand of God got up and left the building, thank you very much.

Chapter Fifteen

Samantha took a long swig of her Diet Coke and said, "Well, that sucked." She sat back in the booth deflated and stared out the window, watching the cars go by outside. I had to agree with her. She and David had worked to put together a meeting with the man they thought would ride in and save the day, the Hand of God no less. But instead, here she was stuck with a man who was only there so that in less than twenty-four hours, he could trade her in for someone else's damaged soul.

When you consider her main confidant had been tortured and brutally murdered, her cover blown, and the Hand of God brushed her off, then my day didn't look so bad. Of course, the night was still young.

She turned back to me and said, "So it's you and me, Vic. The Hand of God is out. How 'bout you? Still willing to help?"

"Sure, why not. I don't have anything planned until six tomorrow night. Until then, I'm free."

This got me another eye roll, which women seem to be really good at when I'm around. I was trying to lighten the mood, but she seemed almost blasé about the possibility that I might trade her in. I know I didn't feel that way, with my stomach in knots just thinking about it.

I said, "What do you want to do next?"

"Well, let's take another look at those documents on your phone Rebecca sent you. Do you know anything about computers?"

I got my iPhone back out and said, "Not much. I know how to turn them on and use the Google Machine part. And I know how to look for deleted items and search through email folders. That's how I found you, by the way. You didn't delete the email of your meeting tonight. Nice apartment."

She hit me hard on the shoulder. "You broke into my apartment and went through my computer?"

"Yep. And all your drawers. I was in a hurry, so I had to just dump the stuff on the floor. Things aren't quite as neat as you left them." This got me an eyebrow raise. "I did keep my eyes mostly closed while dumping out your underwear drawer." The eyebrow went higher. "I did try and help out, though. I put a whuppin' on J.B. and his boys when they broke in right after I did. Oh. And we sort of broke some furniture during the fight. Sorry about that, Chief."

"Anything else?" she asked, giving me the kind of stare my mom would use when she and I both knew I'd been caught breaking house rules.

"No, that's pretty much it. For future reference, I'd make sure and delete any email you don't want others to read. Just saying."

She shook her head and shifted her eyes back to the parts list again, embarrassed. "It's not like I've ever tried to disappear before. I'm kind of new at this."

I said, "Not bad for a first effort. And let's face it, they did send a pro like me to find you. So you didn't have much of a chance anyway. You've been spending the thirty million, haven't you? Everything in your apartment is brand new. And the Mercedes. It threw me off at first. That and the fact you had no pictures on the walls."

"Yeah, I spent some of the money. But the rest is hidden. I plan on donating it to different charities, as soon as I can figure out how to do it so it doesn't come back on me. The Church will never get their money back." She pointed to the phone and said, "This is all gibberish to me."

"Hang on. We're making this too hard on ourselves. I know somebody who's good at this computer crap."

I tapped over to my contacts and pulled up the number for Kurt Pervis. I use Kurt when I need some minor hacking or research done and I don't have the time or expertise to do it myself. In his mid-twenties, Kurt worked for the local cable company doing tech support during the day. A borderline genius, he never managed to make it in the corporate "tech world" because of his reputation for not playing well with others and having the social skills of a ten year old. On the phone, one on one, he's fine. But in social situations, such as dealing with co-workers? Not too good. He typically spends eight hours a day at work wearing a headset and talking to strangers. And during his break? He reads, keeping to himself.

I hit send on the number and after a few rings he said, "What the hell do you want, Vic. It's late on a Friday night and I have three women over here. You're interrupting my groove, man."

"Yeah, right. Put the blow up dolls down for a minute. I got something I want you to look at. I'll text you the images. It's some kind of parts list for building computers. I want you to tell me what kind they're building and anything else you can tell me about them.

"Aw man. I'm really busy. Can't this wait until tomorrow?"

"No way, Kurt. This is a priority job. I have to make some decisions on what I do next based on what you tell me. Don't make me come over there in person. If you do, I'll take a straight pin and pop all your women."

"Yeah, yeah, cut the crap, Vic. I'll do it. No need to yank my chain, man. Text away."

I cut off the call, tapped into my texts from Rebecca and sent the images to Kurt. I added a note asking him to dig into Inspiration Global Software. Kurt had a knack for sifting through digital records to find what others would hope you never noticed. I once joked about him being a part of the hacker group Anonymous and he nearly coughed up a lung, so I wondered how close I got to the truth.

The Dizzy Whizz was getting ready to close so I said to Samantha, "While we're waiting on Kurt to call back, we might as well drive over to Inspiration Global Software and snoop around."

She agreed and we headed out into the night. It was now almost 11 P.M. and the night was cooling off quickly. I opened the door for Samantha and she thanked me as she got in. We could've been just another couple out on a date. Any other time I would have been thrilled to have a woman like her in my car at this time of night.

But not this night, not this girl. Instead of taking home a beautiful babe, I was killing time until I had to decide what I'd do when it came time to trade her in. I pulled out of the parking lot laying down more rubber than I should have, as my frustration showed in my driving.

Inspirational Global Software was located in the heart of St. Matthews, a bustling commercial district made up of shops and old neighborhoods in far eastern metro Louisville. The office was part of an open plan walking mall, with an anchor store being Molly Malone's Irish Pub, my waterhole of choice. The office was tucked into the back of the complex between one shop selling musical equipment and one selling sports gear. Molly's was the only thing open this time of night and they were packed.

I said, "After we take a look, you should let me buy you a drink. Molly's is known for a great selection of beer and Lord knows I could use one right about now."

"First you wanted to kidnap me, now you want to get me liquored up? Maybe I'm not that kind of girl, Vic."

"God, I sure hope you are." I pulled around the complex and parked a couple of blocks down the street. We sat for a moment looking around. It was quiet on this end, well away from Molly Malone's. I couldn't see any security cameras, but I had to operate under the assumption they were there. "Let's go take a look, but keep your head down in case there are cameras."

We got out of the car and I offered her my arm. "We can pretend we're a couple out for a stroll."

With one hand she took my arm. With the other she held her sword case and we walked around to the front of the building. We peered into the front window. I could see a counter with a sliding glass window for a receptionist as well as a door off to the left of the counter. There were two armchairs and that was about it. The walls were a soft powdered blue with a couple of outdoor prints hung here and there.

People were milling about on the mezzanine outside Molly Malone's at the far end of the walk. So, there were too many people watching for me to take a run at the front door. And the back door didn't have a keyhole. It must be secured from the inside. I'd just have to wait till later when people moved inside to get out of the cool night air, to attempt to get inside the front door.

I turned my back to the crowd, slipped the gun and magazine from my pockets, slid the magazine into the gun, and put the gun back into the holster. I said, "I'm guessing the Hand of God doesn't mind me putting myself back together. After all, you have your sword. I'm feeling kind of naked without it—especially since things seem to happen around you. Do you have a problem with it?"

"I don't. Like I told Montoya, I don't think you'll hand me over. So I would rather you be armed and ready than not."

I offered my arm again and we strolled down towards Molly's. "You do realize you're nuts. You only met me a few hours ago, you know nothing about me and yet you think you know whether or not I would trade you to Satan for a family member? While I'm glad you feel that way, are you always this trusting? I still don't know what I'm going to do, yet you think you do? Considering who you're up against, that kind of trust might just get you killed at some point."

She squeezed my arm and gave me a reassuring smile. "You won't do it, Vic. I know you won't."

We walked in and I asked the hostess for my regular table away from the crowd. From my spot I could see both front entrances and the hallway to the backdoor. A DJ was playing some decent rock-n-roll and people were out dancing. There's a huge difference between the Double D and Molly's. For one, you felt like at Molly's you wouldn't catch something that might kill you just by sitting down.

A waitress came to our table and I ordered a Guinness and Samantha had a scotch, neat. We sat in silence until after the waitress brought us our drinks and left.

She twirled her glass around on the table for a moment, watching the amber liquid swirl. She said, "You know, I can't get the image of David being murdered out of my mind. Up until now, this night has seemed so surreal, like it was happening to someone else." She looked at me with those stunning green eyes, pulling me in. Turning serious, she continued, "Let me ask you something, when you killed that man at David's house, and then those two men in the barn, it didn't seem to really bother you. Why not?"

"Truth is, it doesn't. When I was fighting in the Middle East, I was part of a unit that spent most of our time hunting down high value Taliban and Al Qaeda targets. I had no problems with it because of what they did on 9-11. They earned it. Just like the guys I killed tonight. They earned it and I had no choice. They would have killed me for sure, and probably Rebecca, and maybe even you eventually. The one that did bother me was Simpson. He couldn't hurt us. So killing him was pointless. There were other ways to handle him. I know Montoya says it's Old Testament justice, but that was cold-blooded murder. Pure and simple."

Surprisingly accepting, she replied, "Eye for an eye, Vic. He murdered two men tonight, and God only knows how many others. I didn't have a problem with it." I wondered if she really meant it when she downed the shot of scotch in one gulp. "I want to thank you, though. If you hadn't pulled me off that woman I would have kicked her to death. In that moment I wanted nothing more than for her to suffer and die. I'm not sure I could have lived with myself if I'd done that."

Before I could respond, she stood up and slipped off her coat. "Come on, let's dance. With all the death tonight, I want to feel alive." I could now admire her figure fully as her black dress hung nicely in all the right places and the only word that kept going through my mind was "wow". I took my coat off, wreaking of smoke and sulfur, and untucked my dirty shirt to cover my gun.

I followed her out to the dance floor and you could just see all the men in the room turning to watch her dance. The DJ was just finishing up a song I didn't know when we hit the center of the room. Then he jumped right into *Bad, Bad, Leroy Brown*.

Samantha laughed and said, "It's almost like they know you."

"Hell, woman, I think they're singing about you."

And for a few minutes, we lost ourselves in the dancing. No Satan, no Mikey Boy, no death and no lies. I took her hand and spun her around. The Lord works in mysterious ways. Earlier in the day, if you would have told me I'd end the evening at Molly Malone's dancing with a beautiful redhead, I'd have said it would be the perfect evening.

Dancing with Samantha was close. Maybe it was what we'd been through already tonight and the couple of near death experiences. Maybe it was just good old-fashioned chemical attraction, but there was energy to our dancing and I could just feel the intensity rolling off of her. I never wanted a woman more than I wanted her, right then and there.

Yet I couldn't help thinking about an Elvis song: *Hard Headed Woman*. The song was written about temptation, from Eve offering Adam an apple to Samson and Delilah, to Jezebel. I took the job from Satan to save my brother. And here I was dancing and lusting after the one thing that could buy his freedom from Hell. Was this my temptation, my garden of Gethsemane, where Jesus said the spirit is willing, but the flesh is weak? Sister Margaret might be proud of how much I remembered, after all. Elvis, too.

The song ended and most of the people started to head back to their tables. We stood there for a moment, close to each other, when the next song started, *Just the Two of Us* by Bill Withers. I hesitated for just a moment, not sure what to do, when she took a half step forward, put her hands on my chest and moved them up and around my neck.

Like at the Down and Dirty, she made the first move. And like then, I went with it. I slid my hands around to her back and pulled her close, enjoying the feel of her body through the dress. Her body pressed against mine and we moved together. The rest of the room disappeared. She put her head on my shoulder and I leaned my cheek up against her head and breathed deeply, taking her in. For one more song I didn't worry about anything beyond holding her close. I had no idea how many more happy moments I would have. So I put thoughts of my brother and everyone else out of mind and just enjoyed the feel of her against me.

When the song ended she gazed up at me and said, "I don't want to die."

Chapter Sixteen

After the slow dance, we went back to our table and ordered a couple more drinks. I said, "Tell me more about you. Brothers, sisters? Is your mom a member of the Church?"

"Well, I'm an only child and my mother died when I was six years old. She had cancer and it ate her up pretty quick. That's what made my dad listen to Satan in the first place. Dad said Satan came to him one night in a dream and pointed out how God had never answered his prayers, but he would. He explained to him that the Bible was just the victor writing the history and God no longer cared about Man, because if he did care, he would save people like my mother. Satan presented himself as the Angel of Light that would restore man's faith in a divine being. This made the choice for my dad an easy one, from his point of view.

Satan promised to make him rich and famous, and he did. My dad is one of the most famous politicians in the country. The most powerful men and women in the world seek him out and ask his advice. So when it comes down to it, Satan had answered my dad's prayers and kept his promises and God didn't, which is why I think God is dead."

I shook my head. "At least now I can tell you that when the Devil made me the offer to help my brother, I got the impression that God still had him by the short hairs. So if the Devil's reaction is any indication, I think God is still alive. Don't ask me why God didn't save your mother. Probably for the same reason he didn't save my father from the heart attack that killed him, or answer my brother's prayers to become wealthy and famous." I took a moment to down my beer and wave to the waitress for another one for me and a shot for Samantha.

"And I have no clue what that reason is. The problem your dad has, though, is that he did the same thing my brother did. He traded his soul for wealth and power. Those things don't last. A rich man and a poor man take the same things into the great beyond: their souls. The Devil gave me a glimpse of what's in store for my brother. And if the same thing awaits your dad, heaven help him."

This time Samantha sipped her scotch. "Heaven can't save my father. Even if I wanted to save him, he wouldn't listen. He never listens. Dad tells everyone else what to do. You never tell him what to do. After mom died, he shut everybody out."

"Bummer. Even you?"

"Especially me. I was raised by nannies and boarding schools for most of my life. Dad was always out on the campaign trail or traveling to other countries on fact finding trips. Look, I know I make it sound like my dad is an awful person, but he's not. After mom died, he was, I don't know, bitter I guess. When we're together, he's loving enough, in his own way. I know I do love him. That's why I'm trying to stop the Exodus Project. I'm trying to save dad from himself. In a way, I'm trying to save my dad, like you're trying to save your brother."

I didn't bring up the obvious: that her father must have a screw loose if he planned to attack kids and start a holy war. But she was right that our intentions were very much alike and had brought us to this point together. Before I could say anything else my phone rang and Kurt's picture flashed on my screen. I leaned across the table so Samantha could hear, too, and answered it. "What'cha got, brother from another mother?"

Kurt said, "Dude, are you out at a bar? I can hear the music playing. You're out partying while you have me working? That sucks."

"Man, I'm working a case, stopping busting my balls and let me know what you got."

"Fine, whatever. First things first. Seems they have the parts to make five hundred really good computers. Eight gigs of RAM, one terabyte hard drives, top of the line graphics cards, the works. There is one weird thing, though. Each computer has three fans, one over the chip, one blowing out the back, and one blowing air out the top. Pretty standard in some of these higher end computers. But near one of the fans, the front one, they're installing an aerosol canister. It must be some kind of new scent thing. Never heard of it, but I'm curious to see how they tie it in. Be kind of cool if you're playing a game and you could smell the place you're at as well as see it."

I said, "Since the last game I played was Asteroids, I don't think it would help me much."

"Dude, you're so old school. Like *really* old school."

"What else?"

"That's pretty much it on the computers. I've made progress on the company but it's tougher. They're really trying hard to hide the real owners of this thing by using shell and holding companies. The trail has lead me to a holding company in London, but there are more layers for me to get through."

"London, Kentucky?"

"No, dipshit, London, England. But it doesn't stop there. I need to hack into a few more databases and I'll have more information for you later. But definitely pointing to not American owned."

"Huh. Thanks Kurt. Keep digging. This helps out a lot."

"No sweat, Vic. But man you're going to owe me another one, if you know what I mean."

Samantha looked at me questioningly. I winked at her and said to Kurt, "Look man, I set you up the last time and you crashed and burned."

"Dude, she wasn't my kind of woman. It wasn't my fault we didn't work out."

Samantha stifled a laugh. "She was too your kind of woman. She was breathing and had a pulse. And yes, it was your fault it didn't work out. You took her to Wendy's for dinner. Sharon is used to eating at places where they come to your table to take your order, not the other way around. Not exactly a great dinner choice."

"Hey. I had coupons. Still, you'll owe me."

"I'll do what I can, Kurt. The rest is up to you," and hung up.

Samantha asked, "Where did he really take her?"

"To Wendy's. As the man said, he had coupons."

She laughed some more and said, "O.K. I've told you about my family. How about yours? Tell me about your brother."

I told her about Mikey Boy and our upbringing in a blue collar Catholic neighborhood here in Louisville. I talked about my dad, who worked at the Ford plant for nearly forty years before passing away.

"I went to the University of Kentucky and got a degree in history. While I was there, I joined ROTC. After I graduated, I did my four year hitch and liked it, so I re-upped and spent another tour playing in the sand and helping to hunt down Al Qaeda and Taliban wackos. When I got out, I became a bounty hunter. I put what I learned overseas to use back here on this side of the pond."

We spent the rest of the time talking about old boyfriends and girlfriends, the fact that neither of us could seem to keep a relationship going and that we could both agree that lima beans suck. I think we were both just doing our best to put off what we had to do next, but it was time to get moving. The waitress came by, but Samantha and I passed on any more imbibing. I asked her for the check and after she left I said, "I think we need to get inside Inspirational Global Software and see what they're up to."

"Can you get us in?"

"Yes, but we may not have much time once we're inside. If an alarm goes off, or we hear a panel beeping, we get the hell out of Dodge. We don't want to risk getting picked up by the cops. If they've found the van at Rebecca's, then they'll have found David and sooner or later, they're going to fingerprint Dave's house and our fingerprints are going to turn up. Mine are on file with the state as part of my license."

She said, "Mine aren't on file anywhere, but I agree. Now's not the time to be stuck in a holding cell someplace."

The waitress came back and I paid the bill. I helped Samantha put her coat on and then shrugged into mine and we went back out into the night. We walked back past the software company's front door. I stopped and looked at the lock. I told Samantha to keep a watch out and took a set of keys from my inside pocket. I searched around and found what I needed a few doors up at a small flower shop. I picked up a small decorative rock and went back to the front door.

"Since this is a brand of lock I know, I have a bump key that may work."

"What's a bump key?" She leaned up against the wall, blocking the view of anyone watching from down towards Molly's.

"It's a trick I learned from an A.T.F. buddy of mine. Every lock has keys with cuts and grooves to make the tumblers move out of the way to let the cylinder turn. A bump key is a key that is filed down so that the ridges are very short. This allows the key to be inserted all the way in." I sorted out a key and put it in the lock. "Then you pull the key out one notch, apply just a small amount of pressure and hit the key with something hard." I held up the rock. "This bumps the tumblers like billiard balls and allows you to turn the cylinder. If you're lucky." I struck the key with the rock and turned the key. With a click the cylinder turned and the door unlocked.

"Wow. Impressive. Is this how you got into my apartment?"

"Nah. I just picked yours. But let this be a lesson for you, buy better locks."

We entered the office and I closed the door behind us. We stood there for just a minute listening for a beeping from an alarm system, but didn't hear any. We looked around for a security panel and didn't find one. I asked Samantha to watch for cops as I went to the inner door and turned the knob. It opened and I stepped through, once again listening for the sound of an alarm system, but heard nothing nor saw a keypad. I told her to lock the door and join me.

We both moved to the interior office and I flipped on a light switch. There was a counter behind the receptionist's window which held a telephone, a can with a couple of pens and pencils and one of those three hundred and sixty-five day desk calendars, with a different quote from George W. Bush on each page. No one had turned a page since the middle of October and the quote said, *"I'll be long gone before some smart person ever figures out what happened inside this Oval Office."* George W. Bush, Washington, D.C., May 12, 2008. No shit there Sherlock.

The room had two desks, each with a swivel chair and a computer station. There were two doors in the room with one opening to a bathroom and the other to an empty back room with the rear exit. I moved behind one desk, Samantha to the other. A framed photo of two cute kids eating cotton candy sat on the desk, along with a few papers on top stacked neatly. A quick shuffle showed them to be letters thanking Inspirational Global Software for the upcoming donation of the computers and software and several personal notes on how they were looking forward to using the software to teach their children more about the Bible. There were dozens of such letters.

I moved the mouse on my computer and the screen came alive, but asked for a password. No dice. I looked over at Samantha and the computer on her desk showed the same thing. I shrugged my shoulders and started opening drawers. Inside one of them I found a long cardboard box with what I at first thought were business cards, but turned out to be peel-off stickers. They were in some kind of Arabic language that I had no clue how to read.

I showed one to Samantha and asked, "Any chance you read Arabic?"

"No chance. You were the one stuck over there. Didn't you pick up anything?"

"I never talked to them, I just killed them." The only other thing I found in the other drawers was office supplies.

I said, "Looks like to me this is just a front. They must want a physical address in case anyone gets curious and checks them out. My desk has more on it than these two do combined."

"I have to agree. Mine is exactly the same, minus the stickers. I wonder what they say?"

"Sounds like another job for Kurt. Won't he be thrilled." I took a photo of the sticker with my phone and texted it to Kurt, asking for a translation. I got a quick text back saying he wasn't my personal slave, followed by another one that said he was on it.

I sat and thought for a second. "There's something we're missing. I mean, think about it. They have five hundred computers. Let's say they each cost a grand. That would be five hundred thousand. Let's say it costs a hundred each to ship. That's another fifty grand, so a total of about five hundred and fifty thousand dollars. What are they planning on spending millions of dollars on this weekend?"

She started to give me her thoughts but I never heard what she said as a man opened the inner office door, stepped through with his gun raised and shot me in the chest.

Chapter Seventeen

When I picked History to major in at U of K my mother thought I'd end up teaching. Then I joined R.O.T.C. and though it meant I would have to do a four year stint, she never really worried, figuring me for an administrative job. When I was chosen to become a member of a unit which went behind enemy lines, she was terrified; convinced I would die over there. It made things worse because I was never allowed to talk about what I did in service for my country.

When I came home she broke down in tears of joy, like many mothers of returning sons and daughters whose children came back safely. My mom just knew I'd finally get my teacher's certificate and then my master's and become a professor. But me, I craved that adrenaline. If the Army could have promised me other missions where I wouldn't have to spend the next dozen years playing in sand dunes, I might have stayed in and continued the good fight. But they couldn't. And I got tired of finding sand and dirt in places where the sun don't shine.

When I told my mom I decided to become a bounty hunter, she started crying all over again. I made every promise in the book I'd do what I could to stay safe. That included my sworn promise to always wear a bulletproof vest every day I worked. I had mine on that morning and hadn't had a chance to take it off.

Which turned out to be a good thing. I was reaching for my gun when the force of the shot struck me in the chest, knocking me backwards out of the chair and half-way across the floor. It was like somebody took a sledgehammer and pounded me with it. All the air rushed from my lungs, and I fought to stay focused.

Muscle memory reflexes took over and saved my life. Despite the crushing pain, I managed to pull out my gun from its holster. From what seemed like far away, I could hear Samantha yelling at me. As a man moved towards the desk and me, I took aim, and shot him in the ankle. He screamed and collapsed as his ankle disintegrated. The moment he hit the ground, I shot him in the head. It occurred to me, if he'd only shot me like I'd just shot him, I would finally have the answer to the question of which direction I would be heading on that big elevator in the sky.

Samantha crawled to me and ran her hands over my chest, tearing at my shirt, looking for a bullet wound as I struggled, but failed, to get up. She found the vest and said, "I thought I felt one of these while we were dancing. My God Vic, are you alright?"

"Yes," I lied. "Now let me up."

I rose to the level of the desk, my gun hand outstretched as another man stuck his head in the doorway, saw me and ducked back. I shoved Samantha towards the back room and moved to follow her just as the man's hand appeared around the corner and let loose a few rounds in the direction of the desk, luckily striking it and not me. I fired two shots through the wall next to the door and was rewarded with a grunt followed by the sound of a body hitting the floor. Dry wall makes a pretty poor defense against a nine millimeter round.

My chest hurt like hell as I followed Samantha into the back room, closing the door and turning the doorknob lock. It wouldn't slow them down if they decided to kick the door in, but it would give me some warning. The room we were in was about fifteen by fifteen feet and there was not a single stick of furniture in the room. From behind me Samantha said, "I'll check the back door."

I shouted, "No!" But she already had the door open. When she did another man gripped the door from the outside and pulled it further open while taking Samantha by the throat. She swung the sword case up, smashing it into his wrist. He let go of her with that hand, only to snatch her with the other as a second man appeared at the back door and took a shot in my direction. I couldn't shoot back without taking a chance of hitting her, yet I couldn't get closer to help without getting myself shot.

The two of them took hold of Samantha and pulled her kicking and screaming outside. I ran to the closing door and was about to push it open when round after round of gunfire hit it, with one round grazing my arm as it went by. Now my chest had company in the agony department. More rounds were fired from the inside of the office and I retreated to the far corner and hit the ground to avoid being caught in the crossfire as the room exploded with flying plaster.

The shooting stopped and in the ensuing quiet in the room, I could finally hear what the shooters must have heard: sirens. Someone had called the boys in blue. I ran to the back door and opened it just in time to see a black Lincoln Town car go tearing out of the parking lot, taking Samantha with it.

There would be no time to get back and circle the building and to my car before the cops arrived. Sons of bitches. I stuck a finger through the bullet hole in the sleeve of my jacket and probed the wound, but there wasn't that much blood. I took off running across the parking lot and made my way through a series of side streets, putting as much distance between the office and me as I could while furiously thinking what to do about what just happened.

I had to find Samantha again, and soon. And not just for my brother's sake. If they did to her what they did to David-- I let the thought stop there, as it was enough to make me want to throw up. I took a moment to catch my breath and was hit by a new emotion: pure hate.

Many times in my life I've been angry, even severely pissed off. But this was beyond that. I wanted to find them and kill the lot of them: Deveraux, her dad, the guys who kidnapped her, all of them. My phone rang and I yanked it out of my pocket. It was Kurt. I answered with a growl, "What?"

"Dude, we're in deep shit. What the hell have you got me into, Vic?"

I took several deep breaths and tried to calm down. "Where are you Kurt? Like, right at this moment." I could hear background noise and could tell he was in his car.

"Damn it, Vic? Are you hearing me, man? Things have gone to Hell in a hand basket. We need to talk and you need to make things right."

"Kurt, calm the fuck down and answer my question. Where are you?"

"Jesus man, alright. Sorry. I'm just a little wigged out, you know? I'm in the Highlands. I was at that all night cyber café when--"

I cut him off and said, "Pick me up at the corner of Browns Lane and Wetherford. You got it?"

"You mean now? Why don't I just meet you at your place?"

"I'm not at home, Kurt. Just do what I ask please. O.K.?"

"Sure, Vic. Alright. I'm on my way. Geesh. Don't get your panties in a wad."

I leaned against a large maple tree and dry washed my face with my hands. It was now about 1:30 A.M. and the fatigue was starting to catch up with me. Going to Molly Malone's may have been a mistake.

The pain in my chest and arm brought me back to the here and now. I had allowed myself to relax once I had Samantha. And while I hadn't had that much to drink at Molly's, it added to the relaxation and I'd made some poor choices. I should have left Samantha on lookout in case someone had shown up. I should have done more to protect her and instead I only added to the body count while allowing her to be taken.

I did my best to calm down and think while waiting for Kurt. It took him about ten minutes to get there. He pulled up in a blue Toyota Sienna minivan. Most bachelors drive a muscle car. Or at least a nice sedan. Not our boy Kurt. He said he bought it from a friend who offered it to him dirt cheap. When I tried to explain chicks don't dig minivans unless they have kids, he just blew me off. Right now, I didn't care. I came around to the driver's side and he rolled his window down.

"Where's your car?" he asked.

"Scoot over. I'm driving." I opened the car door and he just looked at me. "Kurt, move to the passenger seat, please." I'm not sure what my face looked like, but his reply died on his lips. He unbuckled his seat and scrambled over to the other seat.

I got in and adjusted his seat some. Kurt wasn't what you'd expect when you hear that he's a computer geek who has trouble getting dates and can't keep a girlfriend. At six feet tall, lean swimmer's build, sandy brown hair and chocolate brown eyes, his male-model good looks made every woman notice him when he walked into a room.

His problem was when he opened his mouth. Women, unfortunately, noticed that, too. He had a knack for saying the wrong things at the wrong time. Invariably, when Kurt was alone with a member of the opposite sex, he'd freeze up.

Good thing tonight he and I were not going date hopping, though we were after women. Or at least, one woman. "Jesus Vic, what's happened? No, wait. Let me tell you what happened with me first."

"Hold up, Kurt. You have your laptop with you, right?" The man never went anywhere without it.

"Yes, but that's part of what I need to tell you--"

I cut him off again and said, "In a minute. Get it out and find me the address for Winston Reynolds. Young guy, around twenty-three or twenty-four years old."

He reached around his seat and got his backpack, then pulled out a net book with a satellite connection. In just a couple of minutes he had the machine fired up and an address for Winston. "Why are you looking for him?"

"He has something I need." I knew the part of town Winston lived in and headed that way. "Now, Kurt, what's got a bug up your ass?

"Dude, let me tell you. To dig deeper into Inspirational Global Software, I needed to hack into a few databases. I don't like to do that at home, so I went to Bytes Me, that all night cyber cafe on Frankfort Avenue. Anyways, I was there and I hacked into a business database in London for corporate filings. That led me to other companies and other databases. I ended up in one in Saudi Arabia.

That's when I got to the end of the line on who really owns Inspirational Global Software. A man named Fazil Al Haqar. And Vic, this is a very, very bad man. He's on the terrorist watch list. He's Al Qaeda's point man when it comes to chemical and biological weapons. Our government wants him in the worst sort of way."

Turns out Kurt didn't have to tell me who Haqar was. I'd heard of him. He was one of the men we tried to track down when I was with my unit in Afghanistan. We had a list, kind of like the deck of cards used for Saddam Hussein and his henchmen. Haqar was a high value target we never could find. We thought he was killed by a drone strike in Helmand Province, but we missed him.

Kurt continued, "And then I ran O.C.R. software on that image you sent me, the one in Arabic. Once I did that, I used Arabic translation software and was then able to read the damn thing. It said, "Blessed be to Allah. The infidels in the West now know what it is like to lose innocents. Let this be a warning. Stay out of Muslim countries. Leave the Middle East and never return."

"Vic, the company is owned by a terrorist. And that's not what's got me scared shitless. The program I use to do my hacks has built-in sniffer alarms. They started going off while I was trying to run down more info on Haqar. I panicked and shut down my connection before they could find me. Or so I thought. I left the café and drove over to the Thornton's across the street. While I was gassing up, several cars came flying up to Bytes and a bunch of men got out wearing suit and ties. They just wreaked Feebs. Jesus Vic, they were there less than ten minutes after I'd gotten out of my chair. What the hell have you got me mixed up in?"

Hell, Kurt. I was on a trip to Hell and it seemed I was taking him along for the ride.

Chapter Eighteen

I gave him the condensed version, leaving out Satan, vampires and devil worshipers. Which meant I told him that I'd been hired to find a girl and that in doing so I'd uncovered a plot to attack Christian schools with a computer virus. I told him the bad guys had gotten wind of the investigation and had captured Samantha and that I planned on getting her back. While not quite the truth, it was not quite a lie. If he asked me about the other stuff, I'd tell him. For right now it was better that he not know what could definitely kill him.

The longer I talked, the paler Kurt got. When I finished, Kurt said, "Holy shit, Vic. I'm happy to help, but you're into really heavy stuff man. Have you, uh, hurt anybody tonight?"

I shot him a look that made him raise his hands in surrender and take the question back. He put Winston's address into his GPS and a few minutes later we were there. Winston lived in a ranch house located in a nice older neighborhood on the city's Southside. I parked in the street a few houses down and told Kurt to sit tight.

There were several street lights to see by as I walked up the driveway. I didn't see the Cadillac, but there was a Ford Mustang in the driveway. It was now almost 2 A.M. and the neighborhood was quiet. I stepped up onto the porch and rang the doorbell a couple of times.

It took a bit, but I could hear someone coming to the door. The porch light came on and I could see someone look through the peephole. There was a pause, but the door opened. Winston looked at me with one hand on the door knob and one behind his back. I held both my hands open at my sides, showing him I didn't have a weapon.

The side of his face showed a mark where I'd slugged him. One didn't have to be a psychic to know he wanted nothing more than to beat me down like I had him.

"They're dead, aren't they?" He asked this in a monotone. Like I said, he was smart, and he knew the answer to his question, but he had to ask it nonetheless.

"Yes. Both of them. That's why I'm here. I need your help."

He shook his head very slowly. "J.B. always said you had balls. But you're something else, Vic. I think the best thing you can do is take your sorry ass off my property and get the hell out of here."

"No can do, Winston. I need help and you're the only one that can do it. You want to let me in so we can talk about it or do you want to keep this up on your porch?"

He looked up and down the street, taking his time. "I ain't letting you in this house. No chance in hell. You got something else to say, then say it."

"Fair enough. The men that killed J.B. and the other guy, what was his name?"

"Ian. Ian Adams. Good kid."

"I'm sure. The men that killed the two of them also tried to kill me. Several times tonight, as a matter of fact. They're the men that hired both J.B and me to find the girl. They followed us there and even though J.B. told him the girl was close, they shot him and Ian like rabid dogs. They didn't deserve that. They now have the girl. I plan on getting her back and make them pay for what they did to J.B. and Ian."

"Shit man. You want the bounty that bad? It ain't worth it."

"It's not about the money. They set J.B. and me up against each other and planned on killing us instead of paying up. These are very bad men, Winston. I've since found out they plan on attacking kids and I won't let them get away with it."

The news about attacking kids made him stop and think. I didn't tell him that it would be with a computer virus, but then again, I didn't care. I just needed his help. "What do you want me to do?"

"You guys used a Spark Nano GPS device to find us. I found it before we left the farm under my back bumper. Just before they took the girl, I slipped the tracker into her coat pocket. I need the remote you used to follow us to now find her. It would be great if you joined in and helped me with the payback, but at the very least, I need to know how to follow that GPS tracker."

My brother always told me you gotta have a backup plan. When I helped Samantha on with her coat at Molly Malone's I dropped the tracker into her pocket. I felt like a real douche bag doing it, but I had no idea if she would change her mind and bolt on me. I had to hedge my bets. Turns out it was the right thing to do.

"Man beats the crap out of me then asks me for help. Why should I?"

I took a step closer to him and growled, "Because the sons of bitches must pay. For J.B, for Ian, for the girl and for others they've killed tonight. And, so help me God, they will. You can pretend this doesn't affect you, but it does. They took something from you tonight and you need to take it back."

Winston didn't back down when I invaded his personal space. "Maybe it's time to go to the cops on this. It's gone from bad to royally fucked up. Let them wind things down. If she's been kidnapped, they can even bring in the Feds."

No doubt Winston was right. Hell, it was the same advice I gave to Samantha earlier in the evening. Bringing in the cops now would be the smart thing to do. Things were spiraling out of control. But the moment I did that, I would be on the hook trying to explain why I'd killed four men tonight. Self-defense might work. Might not. But either way, my brother was dead. I had climbed out on a very thin limb that could break under me at any time, but I couldn't stop.

"I'm a bounty hunter. I don't go to the cops for help. Besides, just how would you explain what you and J.B. were doing? Or me, for that matter. We didn't have a warrant to track down Samantha. That's kidnapping. I had my reasons for taking the job. They have something on my brother and I've been trying to get him off the hook. I know J.B. was a good guy, so what did they offer him to take the job?"

"A million dollars. I told him it wasn't worth it, but he took the job anyway. J.B. has his kids in private school. Bills have been piling up. He needed the extra cash. So we took the job. Cost him his life. Like I said, wasn't worth it."

"If he hadn't sent you over to the mansion, you'd be dead right now," I said. "And I'd be avenging your death along with theirs. You don't want to go with me, fine. Just tell me how to find her and I'll get out of your hair."

He looked at me for awhile longer, thinking. Finally he said, "Wait here." He closed the door and was gone for a couple of minutes. When the door opened again, he had a dark red University of Louisville jacket on.

"The info on the tracker is in J.B.'s Caddy, so I'll come with you. Besides, someone has to keep you from getting your ass shot off," he said. "But I'm doing this for J.B. and Ian. When this is over, I'm going to kick your behind for cold cocking me."

"You're going to try and kick my behind. Won't be any different when it's a fair fight. But thank you. I mean it. Thanks."

I offered him my hand and he took it. I led the way back to the van and opened the passenger door. I said, "Kurt, Winston. Winston, Kurt." I nodded with my head and said to Kurt, "Now get in the back seat."

"Come on, dude. It's my car. If I don't get to drive, at least I get to ride shotgun."

"Fine, you tell Rosa Parks here to ride in the back of the bus." I went to the driver side while Winston didn't say anything, just stood there. Kurt said, "Right. My bad. Sorry."

Kurt grabbed his computer, got out and opened the sliding side door and got in. Winston hopped into the passenger seat and I asked him, "Where to?"

"J.B.'s Caddy is at my uncle's house in his garage. I told him I needed to stash it for a bit." He gave me directions. "Now tell me what the hell is going on."

I did so and, like I did for Kurt, I left out the part about the Devil and my brother's soul contract, just telling him that they had him and planned on killing him if I didn't help out. I gave him a run down about what took place at the farm, how J.B. and Ian were killed, and how I took out two of the four guys.

"There's another player in this, however. Samantha, that's the girl's real name, and the reporter, had scheduled a meeting with a man they thought would take on the bad guys for them. Lucky for us, he was outside the Double D when you guys were there, heard you discussing the job and followed you, first to Phoenix Hill, then to the farm. He took out the other two of their men, including the one that shot J.B and Ian. He might be able to help us if we can find out where she is."

Winston listened to the whole thing without interrupting. When I was finished, he asked the same question we all did when this started. Why did they want her? I didn't see telling him would hurt and it might even keep him involved. "She stole thirty million from them. She knew they needed the money for the Exodus Project. She figured no money, no project. The way they've been after her, seems she was right."

"That's a boatload of cash," Winston said. "But it sounds like this is like stealing from the Mafia. They can't go to the cops to get their money back, but they don't mind killing people if they have to. Shit, sends a message. Fuck with us and you pay with your life. We do this, Vic, they're going to be coming after us hard."

"You got a problem with that?" I asked.

"Nah. You do our kind of work, they always be people wanting payback. Let them try."

"That's the way I feel. Up to now, they've been driving the bus. Now, it's time for some of their own medicine. Payback's a bitch."

Kurt said, "Uh, guys? I'm really not into hell-bent Satanists wanting to come after me. Anyway, we can keep me out of this whole payback's a bitch part?"

I said, "Come on, Kurt. The chicks love bad boys. Think of what this will do to your reputation."

He said, "I'm thinking more about what it will do to my lifespan. But while you two have been getting all buddy-buddy, I've been thinking about a different approach with this Inspirational Global Software side of things. I found a Catholic school outside Atlanta and hacked into their systems. First, I cracked open their web servers. Luckily they've got one of those rolling message ads on their main page so I modified it to look for an inbound request from the IGS domain. It will load up a nasty little bug I concocted on any user's machine coming to the page from the Inspirational Global Software network.

"Next, I got into their email server and uploaded a script that will allow me to send mail from the school President's account and will reroute any incoming email from IGS to a fake email account I setup on another service. With all that in place, I fired off an email to IGS from the school president saying how he heard about the contest from another school and how interested he was in what they were doing and to please consider them for the program. I then included a link to the page containing the bug. Once loaded, that baby will route any traffic from that computer back to me—via a very circuitous route, of course. With any luck I'll be in the Inspirational Global Software network in no time."

I looked at Winston and asked, "Did you get any of that?"

Winston said, "Yeah. They click on the link and they're fucked."

I laughed and said, "Any help would be appreciated, Kurt." I couldn't blame him for worrying about his own ass. If the Church found out he's involved, I had no doubt just what action they'd take, based on tonight's events.

We made it to Winston's uncle's house. He owned a couple of acres in a more rural part of the county. Winston called ahead to let him know we'd be headed to the garage and that he might take a few other things while we were there. I didn't ask what "things," as I would find out soon enough.

The garage turned out to be as big as the barn on the farm where Rebecca lived. Winston had me back up through the wide double doors then he hopped out and opened them and motioned me back, guiding me into the barn, parking next to the Caddy. He closed the doors and Kurt and I got out of the van. Winston motioned us to follow him to a door towards the back of the garage.

He took out a key ring, selected the right one and unlocked the door. He opened it and turned on an inside light. We went down about a dozen steps, revealing what could only be Rambo's wet dream. One side of the room was lined with display shelves with several rows of automatic weapons, side arms and even a crossbow. The other side had boxes of ammo, grenades and several other boxes of weapons.

"Who the hell is this guy?" I asked. I walked over and looked at one of the shelves and found flash bang and concussion grenades. "How did he get all this stuff?"

"My uncle is convinced one day the Chinese are going to invade the United States and try and take all our guns away. Or the Federal government is going to outlaw all guns and come and take all our guns away. Or take your pick. Someone is always coming to take his guns, and he plans on making his last stand from here. He has friends in the militia movements and picks up what he needs from them."

I whistled while turning around looking at all the firepower in this one room. If the world ever started to come to an end, I wanted to come make my stand with Winston's uncle.

"What can we take?" I asked, picking up a couple of each of the types of grenades.

"He said we can help ourselves and bring back the guns when we're done with them. I told him we'd pay to replace anything we use and can't bring back, so, help yourself. It's your bank account funding this trip.

Great. If I managed to save Samantha, save my brother, save myself, and live to see another day, I would have to hit her up for an expense account. I pocketed grenades and then checked out my choices of sub-machine guns.

I had a choice of several versions of the MP5, a 9mm sub-machine gun used by Navy Seals and one we used in Afghanistan, so I was familiar with it. It has a closed bolt action which means little kick. I settled on an MP5K with a Gemtech suppressor and a couple of boxes of the Remington 9mm Luger subsonic ammo. This time the Church wouldn't have the edge in firepower. And as quiet as this baby would be, they wouldn't hear it coming either.

Winston loaded up in a similar fashion and we took the gear, along with a duffle bag to put the stuff in, and loaded it into the back of the van. He then went over to the Caddy and pulled out a net book, powered it up and opened a document. "We use the Spark Nano. All you need is the sign on name and password. J.B. kept the info in this Word doc. The sign on name is JBRocks and the password is KissMyAss."

Kurt snickered at the password and opened up his own laptop, went to the BrickHouse Security site, and typed in the login and password. A moment later, a map appeared on the screen with a blue dot showing where the tracker had stopped.

Deveraux and the Church had been playing by their rules. Time they learned a lesson. Rules change.

Chapter Nineteen

The BrickHouse security site showed a Google Earth view of where the tracker was at any given moment, and with any luck, where Samantha was currently located. The map showed a house, with several outbuildings, surrounded by nothing but pasture. Kurt clicked on the blue icon and it popped up an address. He then used routing software to pinpoint where it was in relation to us.

"Looks like it's just outside of La Grange, out Highway 53. We can be there in about a half hour. And there's a gravel farm road that runs behind the property. You might be able to approach it from that direction."

Now we were doing things that I was good at. We had a target, knew where they were and it was time to storm the castle, rescue the damsel in distress and make the bad guys pay. I looked at my watch and saw it was just after three in the morning. I looked at Winston and asked, "Are you ready for this?"

"Yea, just let me get a few more things out of the Caddy. He went to the rear of the Cadillac and brought back a smaller duffel. He said, "Three pairs of night goggles, three flashlights and a few other things that might come in handy."

"Sweet. Let's go kick some ass."

I got back behind the wheel and started the van while Winston opened the doors of the garage, then shut them behind us after I pulled out. Kurt was typing away on his laptop from the back, yawning the whole time. Winston hopped back into the van and I put the address of the target into the Garmin and we hit the road.

In my rear view mirror, I could see a porch light turn on and an elderly black man, step out onto the porch. He was dressed in pajamas, but had a gun belt around his waist with a couple of hand guns on each side. He watched us pull out and then headed towards his garage.

Kurt said, "I've looked up the address we're headed to and it's owned by one of the shell companies that owns IGS. So it's definitely part of the Church's network. I can tell you they're current on their taxes and utility bills, but not much else."

I asked, "Can you tell if the bad guys made any other stops on the way?"

Kurt hit a few keystrokes and said, "They made one stop, a house in the Cherokee Park area. One sec' and I'll tell you who owns it." A few moments later he said, "It's owned by Lincoln Townsend."

I nodded. "The computer guy. He's the Church's version of you."

"Not a chance he's as cool as me. Let me see what I can find on the dude."

I was really starting to feel my ass drag from the lack of sleep. I whipped into a gas station and got coffee for Winston and me, heavy on the cream and sugar, and a Diet Dr. Pepper for Mr. Watching-His-Girlish-Figure in the back. The man lived on Diet D.P. I also grabbed some bottled waters and snack bars for later, as well as several energy drinks in case we needed them.

The three of us were quiet as we rode into the countryside. We took I-71 north until we reached La Grange, slipped off the exit and made our way up the hill and through town. La Grange started as a railroad town, with the buildings along main street hailing from the early twentieth century. Today, most were antique shops, specialty stores, restaurants, an art gallery and even a publishing house. But at this hour the town was ghostly quiet.

We crossed the tracks and passed through the other side of town and into rural farmland, with a light fog forming in the cool November air. Kurt had his Garmin set to use a British voice and she happily told us we were point two miles from our destination.

Kurt said, "The farm road will be coming up on the right."

I said, "Let's continue past the place and turn around where the highway dead ends into Highway 42. You and Winston keep an eye out as we go by, though it's not like you're going to see anything in the dark."

And I was right. The house sat far enough back off the road that no lights were visible. This was probably the point. We made it to the end of the highway and turned around at the T. As we approached the gravel road, I killed the lights and made the turn. I rolled down my window, Winston did the same, and we drove slowly, listening to the country night sounds. I stopped when Kurt said we were about even with the farmhouse, which was still a good three quarters of a mile away across open fields, did a quick three point turn in the narrow road and stopped the van.

I had him turn off the dome light and the three of us got out. We left the doors ajar and the van's sliding side door open—just in case we needed to make a quick dive and drive getaway. There was a thin strip of trees at the edge of the road between us and the property, with a three line barbed wire fence.

I said to Kurt, "Get behind the wheel, leave the windows down, but the motor off. I'll call or text you to let you know we are headed back to the van. Don't be a hero. If you think Winston and I aren't coming back, take off. Call the cops. Tell them everything you know. But wait as long as you can, do you understand?"

"Got it, man. No worries on the whole hero thing. I like you. And Winston seems O.K. But, dude, I'm kind of against the whole dying part."

I slapped him on the back, which sent him staggering a couple of steps. "Just be ready to haul ass when we get back here."

Winston and I went to the rear of the van and opened the back door. We opened the two duffle bags and started taking out what we'd need for the raid. Winston took out a pair of thermal night vision goggles, handing me one. I put the goggle harness on my head, adjusted it for my larger head, and flipped them up.

He then took out two Bluetooth earpieces which we synced with our phones. Next we turned our phones on vibrate and dimmed the screens. Finally, we took out the MP5Ks and attached the suppressors. I handed him an extra clip, picked up one of my own and loaded the ammo, while he did the same. He asked, "How do you want to play this?"

"Let's approach them from two sides. Since you're younger and in better shape, I'll let you hoof it around to the far side of the house. If you see anyone on guard duty, let me know, and I'll do the same. I'll call you and we can leave the call open."

He said, "No problem, ole' man."

"If there's no one out watching, then we'll move in closer and assess."

I handed him a flash bang. "We try to hit them, front and back, at the same time. But don't be squeamish if someone points a gun in your direction. Take them out. These guys won't hesitate to blow your ass away."

Winston said, "You don't have to worry about that with me. Let's get this party started."

I handed him a couple of snack bars and a bottled of water. "We may have to watch for a bit, so just in case."

He took the snacks and water, stuffed them in his coat pockets, slung the gun strap over his shoulder, put on his night vision goggles, grabbed a fence post, hopped over and was off at a steady jog. I did a quick fist bump with Kurt and off I went into the dark night, right behind Winston.

I saw Winston swing out wide so as to not risk being seen from the house. Clouds were beginning to move in and the moon kept popping in and out from its hiding place. As long as the bad guys weren't looking out with night vision or thermal goggles of their own, we were pretty safe from detection.

There were several small hills between me and the house, and as I eased up on one, I could clearly see the house in the thermal image. I lay flat on my stomach and scanned the surrounding area. There were two out buildings. One was a small shed. The other appeared to be a detached garage. I could see the back of the house and there was one back porch light on illuminating a small area. I watched for several minutes, but saw no movement. I looked off to my right and could just make out Winston moving to the other side of the house.

I took out a snack bar and devoured it, then washed it down with some water. The quick buzz from the coffee was starting to wear off, so I pulled an energy drink from my pocket and downed that as well, all the while, watching the house.

Winston said softly in my ear piece, "There's a man walking the perimeter of the house. He has no night eyes and is smoking a cigarette. He will be coming into your line of vision shortly." And right on cue, he came around the house to where I could see him. His cigarette glowed brighter as seen by my goggles. I pushed them up as he walked into the light and stopped to look around.

The man was ruining any night vision he might have had by standing in the light. Rookie. He was wearing the coveralls that I was now beginning to think of as their uniforms. He had an M16 slung over around his neck and cradled it in front of him. After a moment, he started back on his rounds and I alerted Winston.

There were several lights on in the house, but the curtains were drawn and I couldn't see anything. Winston said, "I see a black Lincoln Town car in the driveway. Has to be your guys."

I agreed. "When he circles past you again, move in closer to the house. I'm going to take care of him on this side. We're not waiting any longer."

"Roger that," Winston replied.

I couldn't wait longer even if I'd wanted to. I kept thinking of what these guys might be doing to Samantha and I could feel the anger rising inside me like a tidal wave threatening to sweep all other thoughts away. I pulled the goggles back down, moved even closer and lay back down in the grass and waited. Sure enough, the man once again stopped in the circle of light. I pushed the goggles back on my head, and steadied the guns site center mass on my target. I took in a breath, let it out slowly and squeezed the trigger.

There was a soft pfpt from my gun, followed by the man being thrown backwards, then hitting the ground. I was up and running before he even landed. I pulled the goggles back down and said to Winston, "One down, move in."

I got up and sprinted towards the man I'd just killed. I gave Montoya grief for killing Simpson, yet I'd just killed a man without giving it a single thought. I had no clue if the man had ever hurt anyone or was just a hired hand. And I didn't care. He was in the way and I needed him removed, so I shot him. End of story. What was my lack of caring doing to my own soul? I told myself I was doing it for the right reasons, that I was fighting on the side of the righteous. But I had my doubts.

For the moment, I pushed all such thoughts aside, and when I reached the man I grabbed him by the shoulders and dragged him around the house and into the deeper shadows. He looked young, maybe early twenties. He should have been out painting the town instead of lying dead in someone else's yard. Definitely sucked to be him. I pulled the M16's strap up and over his head, then put it over mine, pushing it so it hung down my back. I ran my hands over his coveralls, feeling for anything else that might come in handy or help us, but found nothing.

Winston said, "I'm by the front door. Let me know when you're ready."

I was about to respond when the back door opened and someone called out, "Yo, Janssen."

I moved to the corner of the house and flattened against the wall, holding my gun against my chest. The voice said, "Janssen! Answer me for Christ's sake."

The man was moving towards me and I could see his shadow, thrown by the bulbs light, stretching my direction and moving closer. Just as he reached the corner I stepped forward and put the muzzle of my MP5 against his forehead and said, "You so much as sneeze and I'll clear out your sinuses permanently, got it?"

The man nodded and I motioned him towards the darkness of the deeper shadows at the side of the house. I said to Winston, "I have one of them hostage. Hold tight while I ask this guy a few questions.

"Roger."

I turned the man around and put my gun to the base of his skull. I said, "Answer my questions softly and quickly. Do you have the redhead girl inside?"

"Yes. She's there. Aw, shit man, you killed Janssen?"

"Without even blinking. And I'll do the same to you if you piss me off. How many men left inside?"

"Three more. Two guys in the living room watching TV, one with the girl in the bedroom."

I could feel my face flush. "If you guys have hurt her, so help me God, I'll rip all of you to pieces. What, you guys taking turns?"

The man said "No man, it's not like that. She's tied to the bed, but we haven't touched her. I swear to God, no one's done anything to her."

"If I get in there and find out you lied, shooting you is the best you can hope for."

"I'm not lying, man, she's out. The only thing we did was give her something to make her sleep. She was fighting too much and we needed her to calm down. So Bautista made her take a couple of sleeping pills. That's it, I swear it."

"Who's Bautista? And is Deveraux here?"

The man licked his lips. He said, "Bautista is in charge here at the house. And no, Deveraux isn't here yet. He'll be here first thing in the morning."

"Is the front door locked?"

"No. Not with all of us here. Besides, we could see someone

coming up the drive from quite a ways off. Or so we thought."

I asked the guy for the floor plan inside and found out the others were watching TV in the front room, where the front door is located and the bedroom where they were keeping Samantha was down off the kitchen.

I relayed that info to Winston and said, "I'm going to take this guy in through the back door. I'll toss a flash bang where they're watching the boob tube and you come through and take them down. I'll head to the bedroom and get Samantha. Ready?"

"Lead the way, old man. Hope you don't have to stop and take a leak along the way."

"You need to learn to respect your elders."

I grabbed the Church guy by the scruff of the neck and walked him to the backdoor. "If you don't want to end up like Janssen, then do exactly what I tell you. I have no problems shooting a man in the back. What's your name?"

"Troy."

"O.K. Troy. Whether you live or die will be decided in the next couple of minutes. It's up to you."

I told him to open the back door and we walked into a mudroom that was just off the kitchen. I could hear a TV in another room and I had Troy stop while I took out the flash bang. I pulled the pin and then prodded him with my gun to move forward. The kitchen had an opening straight ahead and a hallway that ran to my right with several doors on the left side, one to the right and one straight ahead.

I tapped Troy on the shoulder and pointed down the hall, and mouthed which one. He mouthed end of the hall, I pointed him towards the front room and just before he reached it I shoved him forward into the room and tossed in the flash bang.

There was a brief second and then a thundering boom, accompanied by a flash of bright light, hence the flash bang name. It was strong enough that plaster fell from the ceiling. The front door crashed open as I took off down the hallway.

I was half-way down the hall when the door on the right opened and a man came hurrying out still zipping up his pants. To say he was surprised to see me is something of an understatement. He was almost as tall as me, but so skinny that if he turned sideways I wouldn't have been able to see him.

I give the guy credit. He took a swing and landed a left to my chin. Too bad for him he did nothing more than hurt his hand. I grabbed him by the neck and drove his face into the wall, making a nice face print in the dry wall and breaking the guy's nose, as blood came gushing out. I was about to toss him out of the way when the door at the end of the hallway opened, with a guy standing behind it holding a handgun.

I tossed Slim down the hallway as the other guy opened fire, hitting Slim several times and spinning him around. I let loose a short burst with the MP5 and the shooter went down. I'd now killed as many men in one night as I had in any single night fighting for my country.

I made it to the bedroom and glanced quickly inside. Samantha was tied to the headboard of a queen sized bed, sound asleep despite the loud action going on in the house. She was still wearing her black dress, but her shoes were missing. Her coat was tossed on the floor next to the bed and her sword case was open with the sword still inside, sitting on a chest of drawers. I cleared the room by checking a bathroom and a closet, then went back to check on Winston.

He had Troy and an older Hispanic man handcuffed with plastic ties, hands behind their backs, lying on their stomachs. Both still looked dazed.

Winston said, "Hope you don't mind, but I didn't just go off and shoot these two."

"No worries, I only shoot them when I have to." But I was lying. I wished he had just shot them. I wanted them all dead. That was the thought rolling through my brain and banging to get out. Kill them all. I said, "See what you can get out of these two, I'll be right back."

In the kitchen I found a knife and went back to the bedroom and cut Samantha loose. I paused just a moment to watch her lying there, sleeping peacefully, and several what ifs passed through my mind, about what life with a woman like her would be like. I took a deep breath and pushed such thoughts aside. I shook her for a bit and she started to wake up. I said, "Come on, Samantha, we've got to get moving." The ropes had chafed her skin where she must have fought being restrained. I lifted her up into a sitting position and her eyes fluttered open. She said, "Victor? You're here? How did you find me?"

"Magic. Now let's get you up and out of here. Come on."

With my help she got out of bed and I picked up her coat and slipped it on her shoulders. I looked for her shoes but came up empty. I closed her sword case and brought it with us. She stopped to look at the man lying in a growing pool of blood on the bedroom's hardwood floors. She said not a word, but stepped around him and then over Slim. I put my arm around her waist as we made our way down the hallway to the living room, and she leaned her head against my shoulder then slipped her arm around my waist. I felt a surge of relief go through me now that I had her back.

We had stormed the castle and rescued the damsel in distress. Now we just had to get her out and someplace safe. Question now was would this fairy tale have a happy ending?

Chapter Twenty

Winston said, "So this is the girl everyone wants? I can see why." He smiled and continued, "I've been talking to these two while you were in the back. They had someone watching the office you broke into, just in case you showed up. They were keeping tabs on several different places she might have known about."

"And Deveraux, when is he supposed to get here?"

"Sometime in the morning, but they weren't given a specific time."

I walked over and crouched down next to the man I assumed was Bautista. "Tell me about the Exodus Project."

He said, "I don't know nothin' about that. It's not in my job description."

I rolled him over onto his back, pulled out my 9, forced his mouth open and shoved the gun's muzzle into his mouth. "See, I think you know more than you're saying. So I'm going to ask you again and if you can't tell me about the Exodus Project, I'm going to air out the back of your head and see what Troy can tell me. So let's try this again. Tell me what you know about the Exodus Project."

I took the gun out of his mouth and pressed the muzzle against his forehead. Bautista said, "O.K. Listen, all I know is bits and pieces. They don't share things with the hired help. But I overheard Mr. Deveraux talking about this guy that's flying in today. And that's why they need the girl. They owe him money and I guess she took off with it. So they have to get her to tell them where the money's at. I swear to God that's all I know."

"Why is it you Satanists all swear to God when you get your nuts in a vice? Why not swear by the Lord of the Light Reclaimed?"

"Sir, do not jest about the Lord of Light. He's real. You don't want to invoke his name so lightly."

I stood up and said, "I've met him. I wasn't impressed with Luci. That's what all his BFF's call him."

Samantha was leaning against the door jamb listening to the

conversation and yawning hard enough to make me want to take a nap right there. I took out my other energy drink and handed it to her. "See if this peps you up at all."

She took the drink and downed it while I walked over to a lamp, yanked out the cord and walked over to Bautista and tied up his ankles. Winston did the same to Troy with a telephone line. He asked, "What do you want to do with these two?"

"Leave 'em. Let Deveraux deal with them."

Troy, a panicked look on his face, said, "Take us with you. You can't leave us like this, he'll kill us!"

"True that," I said. "But you should have read the small print when you signed up."

I asked Samantha, "Did either of these guys hurt you?"

She said, "Not much. They weren't exactly gentle when they tied me down, but I'm O.K."

Good for the continued health of Bautista and Troy because I'm not sure what I would have done if she had said they had. I went and looked out the window into the night for a moment. I had to get control of this runaway anger I was feeling coursing through my body. Maybe I was just overly tired, on top of everything else going on. I pride myself on being calm, cool and collected in any situation, but I could feel that calm slipping away and I was struggling to get it back.

I turned to Winston and Samantha. "As much as I would like to stay and wait for Deveraux to show up, there's no telling what kind of help he'll bring with him. So we'd better get out of here."

We went out the front door and I shot the tires of the Lincoln. Winston and I led Samantha back across the fields towards the van. I called Kurt to let him know we were on our way back.

We were halfway across the field when I heard a sound that gave me goose bumps all over my body. It was the howl of a dog, but unlike any I'd ever heard before. I instantly knew how Sherlock Holmes must have felt standing on the moor and hearing the Hound of the Baskervilles.

Samantha said, "My God. They have a Hellhound here. Run!"

The three of us took off at a dead sprint, running as if our lives depended on it. Winston, younger and faster than either Samantha or I, slowed down to keep pace with us. Admirable, but not a good idea. I said, "Don't hold back. Take off and get over the fence, and help Samantha when she gets there."

"Done deal. Don't slow down, old man. I'd hate to have to avenge you, too." And with that, the former All Big East linebacker took off.

I said to Samantha, "How do you kill one of these things? Do I have to chop its head off, too?" The Hellhound howled again and it was definitely headed our way and gaining.

"No, but they're harder to kill than a regular dog, if my father's stories are true."

Great. "Keep going and don't stop." And doing just the opposite, I stopped, turned and waited. I opened her sword case and took out the sword, then stuck it in the soft ground should I need it and tossed the case on the ground.

Samantha stopped and asked, "What the hell are you doing? Come on!"

I turned to look at her just in time to see her eyes go wide. I glanced back to see a dog racing across the field towards us, though calling this a dog is like calling a lion a cat. The thing was huge, larger than a Great Dane and as stocky as a baby bull. Its fur was a midnight black, with eyes that glowed a sickly yellow color, which made it easy to follow as it closed upon the two of us.

"Samantha, if you don't make it to the van I'll be very pissed at you. So would you please run now?"

She let out a tortured moan and then took off. At least there was one woman in the world that did as I asked. I had to wonder if I would get a chance to get used to it.

I reached into my pocket and took out the last flash bang grenade. I wanted to make sure the thing focused on me and not the fleeing woman, so I started whistling and saying, "Here doggy, doggy. Come here, boy. Good doggy."

When the Hellhound was about a hundred yards away, I took careful aim and let him have it with the MP5. The first round or two hit it and it slowed fractionally, then started to weave slightly, making it harder to hit. Damn thing was smart. I hit it a few more times as it got closer, but I couldn't see that I was doing much damage.

I pulled the pin and let the clip go on the flash bang when the thing was only twenty or so yards away. I threw the grenade and said, "Fetch!" The Hellhound growled and caught the flash bang in its mouth and bit down hard. The grenade went off, the blast taking off part of the hound's jaw. An incredibly scary sound came from its throat, somewhere between a howl and a growl. I yelled back at the top of my lungs. Despite losing half its jaw, as it reached me it leaped for my throat.

In one motion I grabbed the sword, fell to my knees and as the Hellhound sailed over me by inches, I rammed the sword deep into its chest. I held on to the sword, with both hands, ripping it from chest to groin. Blood splattered me and burned where it touched bare skin.

The Hellhound collapsed to the ground when it landed, wrenching the sword from my grasp. I emptied the rest of my clip into its head for good measure and the beast stayed down.

I approached the thing cautiously, not wanting to leave Samantha's sword behind. No telling when we might run across another vampire. Other than a few leg twitches, the life had fled the body. I pulled the sword out, the blade blackened, snatched up her case, and jogged after Samantha and Winston.

We needed to skedaddle as someone had to have let the Hellhound loose and I wanted to be long gone before anything else showed up.

As I neared the fence, I saw Winston in the van's side door, weapon aimed back my way. He lowered it when he saw it was me, hopped out and got in the passenger seat. I got in the van, slammed the door shut and Kurt took off down the road.

Samantha wrapped me in a fierce hug, and then kissed me. Unlike the kiss at the Double D, this one set my body on fire. Right then, I'd have walked through Hell wearing a gasoline suit to kick Satan's ass, if she had asked me to. When the kiss ended, she rested her forehead against mine and said, "I knew you would come for me. When they took me, I was terrified they would do to me what they'd done to David. The one thing that helped was I knew you would find me. And you did."

"Sons of bitches needed to pay. And I plan on seeing to it they keep paying."

Kurt hit the highway, switched on the lights, turned left and accelerated back towards La Grange. He asked, "Where to now?"

"Head back to the interstate and into Louisville. I'll think about it as we get closer to town."

I made the introductions and brought Samantha and Kurt up-to-date on what we'd learned from the Church's men. I asked, "Did they say anything to you while they had you?"

"Nothing important. They just told me that Deveraux would be there in a few hours and that I'd better cooperate with him. They made me take a couple of sleeping pills and I was so tired to begin with, I was out before I knew it."

As we approached a rest area, I had Kurt pull in so that we could change places driving—just in case we ran into more surprises. Kurt drove like my grandmother and his idea of evasive driving was never leaving home. I said, "What we need is some rest. Winston, why don't we drop you off at home? Kurt can run Samantha and me back to my car, and then we can cut you lose, too, Kurt. After we get some rest, we can figure out what our next move will be."

When we got to Winston's house, I got out and walked him to his door. "Thanks Winston. J.B. would've been very proud of you tonight."

He nodded and said, "Yeah. I think so, too. Look, Vic, you be careful. You seem to be falling hard for this girl. Don't let it screw with your brain, man. If you can use my help in whatever your brother's into, give me a shout. I'll do what I can. You can keep my uncle's stuff until this is over. Call me later and let me know what's going on."

I said I would and went back to the van. I drove back to my car, and stopped a few blocks down the street to check things out. I told Kurt and Samantha to wait while I went back to get my car.

No one seemed to be around, but I gave the car a quick search, looking for any new GPS tracking devices. Convinced the car was clean, I fired it up, drove back and picked up Samantha and the gear. I rolled down my window and said to Kurt as he got back behind the wheel of the van, "You did great tonight, Kurt. We wouldn't have Samantha back without your help. Go home and get some rest. I'll call you later."

"I have just one question for you, Vic. Does she have a sister?"

"Get the hell out of here. And watch your ass."

We both pulled out and took off. I made a quick stop at the 24-hour Wal-Mart so Samantha could pick up shoes, jeans and a couple of tops and I could buy a T-shirt and change of underwear. I hated to see the black evening dress go and the view that went with it, but I had to think she could wear a burlap sack and look great. I then headed to a low rent motel on the south-side of town. We went inside, paid for a room in the back and within ten minutes had the gear inside and the curtains drawn. I used one of the room's chairs and propped it under the doorknob for good measure.

I told Samantha I was going to take a shower. I smelled like sulfur, and was covered in an assortment of blood, both my own and others. I sat a gun on the nightstand and told her if anything or anyone tried to come through the door, blow it the hell away. I went into the bathroom, stripped down, turned the water on scalding hot, and stepped into the shower. I was bone tired and the adrenaline rush had long since passed.

I leaned my head against the shower wall and tried to think of what we needed to do next. I had to stop charging like the proverbial bull in a china shop and start planning ahead.

I heard the bathroom door open, then the shower curtain slide back and Samantha joined me. It was clear it was her body that made the dress look good and not the other way around. For one of the few times in my life, I was speechless. Our eyes met and hers were full of playfulness. She took the soap from my hand and started slowly lathering my chest as we kissed. My hands slid down her back and around her bottom. The touch of her skin felt electric when her breasts pressed against me. When her hands moved down my stomach and then lower, I took the soap from her hand and set it back on the soap rack.

I turned her around and she put her hands on the wall as I entered her. While we made love, she leaned back against me and ran her fingers in my wet hair as I kissed her neck and shoulders. I'd never wanted a woman more than I did Samantha and from her response, I could tell she felt the same for me.

When we finished, the tiny motel bathroom now felt like a sauna. We took turns drying each other off. She gently stroked the bruise on my chest and the wound on my arm where I'd been shot earlier. She kissed both spots and while I'm not sure they felt any better, I know I damn well didn't care.

We made our way back into the other room, pulled back the bedding and fell into bed together. We made love again, this time in a slow, tender way that was a total contrast to how the rest of the evening had gone. When we finished, she laid her head on my chest and I played with her still damp hair.

She said, "For the first time tonight, I feel safe."

"We should be safe, for a while at least. Why don't you get some rest?"

Whether it was the sleeping pills she'd taken earlier, or just sheer exhaustion, in just a few minutes, she slipped into a deep sleep.

I was awake for quite some time, listening to her breathing, feeling her warm body against mine, thanking God she was still alive. It would be sunrise before long and I had decisions to make.

Chapter Twenty-One

I must have fallen asleep because I was jolted awake by the ringing of my iPhone. I use the old fashioned telephone ring because it's loud. When my eyes opened, I found Samantha sitting on the side of the bed, the blanket pulled around her hips, holding the Spark Nano tracker in her hands. She was staring at it while idly turning it over and over.

I picked up my phone from the nightstand, and seeing the call was from Kurt, answered it, while watching Samantha who kept her back to me.

"Morning. This better be good, Kurt."

"They clicked on the link. You know what that means.

"Yep. They're fucked. What you got?"

"Not on the phone. Meet me for breakfast. Bob Evans over off Hurstbourne Lane. You're buying, big guy."

"You got it, but give me an hour, will you?"

"See you then."

I ended the call and put the phone down. Samantha looked perfect in the muted sunlight coming through the drab curtains of our motel room. I rolled over and trailed my fingers down the curve of her back and caressing the side of her hip.

She said, "I wondered how you found me. I didn't think about it much last night. But this morning, I was curious. And I thought about how the other bounty hunter had tracked us by putting a GPS device on your car. So I checked my coat and found it. When did you put it there?"

"When we left Molly's, when I helped you on with your coat."

She finally looked at me and I saw disappointment. "You didn't trust me, did you?"

"It wasn't a matter of if I did or didn't. It was a matter of I couldn't afford to take the chance you'd bolt. If you took off on me, I would be out of options," Vic said.

"You mean about your brother."

"Yes, that's what I mean. Turns out it's a good thing I did. I don't know if I would have found you otherwise out there in the middle of nowhere."

She nodded. "I know. So I'm saved by a betrayal." She held up her hand to stop me from speaking. "Don't get me wrong. I'm glad you found me. It's just..." She tossed the Spark Nano onto the nightstand and gave me a small sad smile. "It doesn't matter. Thank you."

She leaned down and kissed me and I took her into my arms and we spent the next half hour making love before getting out of bed and getting dressed.

I could tell even during our lovemaking that things had changed. I knew she was upset with me and I couldn't blame her. Yet if I hadn't done what I did, there's no telling what Deveraux might be doing to her right at this very moment. Damned if you do, damned if you don't. And that pretty much summed up the choices I was facing.

I kept asking myself, if you do bad things for a good reason, how are you judged when your eternal soul is on the line? I had killed several men the night previous, so what kind of balance did my scale hold? I had seen the Hand of God kill a man. I presume he had authority to act in God's name. But what about me? If fighting the Church of the Light Reclaimed meant killing people, would I be forgiven?

By the time we left the motel and made it to Bob Evans, we arrived only a few minutes late, arriving a little after 9 A.M., and found Kurt waiting on a bench outside the restaurant, with his laptop on in his lap, typing away. He didn't even see us walk up. I tapped him on the shoulder. "If you keep that up you're going to get that hand disease."

"Carpal tunnel? Even if I do, they make great speech-to-text programs. Let's go in, I'm starving." Captain Literal once again failed to get it.

We were seated at a table in a corner and made small talk until the waitress took our orders. Kurt could barely hold back his excitement. When the waitress left, he said, "Someone clicked on at 6:48 A.M. and that gave me access. I automatically made an image of the hard drive and while that was being done, I had a look around. You said they were expecting someone in town today, right?"

"Yeah. That's why they needed Samantha. Whoever it is, they're paying them the big bucks. Did you find out who?"

"You betcha. I got onto their email server and there were several emails of interest, including an itinerary for someone named Raakel

Korhonen. She's flying in this morning at eleven to Louisville International on a charter flight from Helsinki, Finland."

Samantha asked, "Were you able to find out who she is?"

"Well, that's not as easy as you might think. Both her first and last names are some of the more popular names in Scandinavia. It's like being called Jane Smith here. I did some checking and there are several possibilities. I was high on one that works for a company called Virasynth because I thought it might be a computer company, but it turns out it's not. Wrong kind of bug. So I moved on to the next one who looks the most promising. She works at the Ministry of Defense. I think--"

I said, "Wait. What do you mean wrong kind of bug?"

"She doesn't work for a computer company. Virasynth works with infectious diseases, trying to find things like a vaccine for bird flu, protection against anthrax, that kind of thing."

And then it hit me. It wasn't a computer virus they were buying, but a virus IN the computers. Kurt continued on with his list, but I was no longer listening, as I was thinking about how many people, especially children, they could kill if they unleashed a virus at all those different schools.

"Stop," I said, cutting him off. "I think you were right the first time. Don't you guys see? The one question we've been asking, over and over, is how you start a religious war with a computer virus. The answer is: you don't. But you could if you used a real virus. A highly contagious virus. Those canisters that you said were being built into the computers, the ones that were right next to the computer fans, what if those canisters held a virus set to be blown into the room at a certain time? Like during an academic competition when all those children and their teachers would be gathered around them?"

"Holy shit," Kurt said. "And those stickers you had me translate. That would explain Fazil Al Haqar's involvement. If those computers really did have a virus in them, eventually they'll track back to who owns ISG, just like I did. If each computer had one of those stickers placed inside all holy hell would break loose."

Samantha said, "And that would also explain why they need all that cash. I'd have to think a bio-weapon on the black market would bring tens of millions of dollars."

We stopped talking as our waitress brought us our food. Samantha and Kurt had seemed to lose their appetite, but I dug in. There's nothing like biscuits and milk gravy to get a bounty hunter ready to kick some ass. I said, "Eat up. It could be a long day and you always take nourishment where you can get it."

Samantha said, "So they really are planning to kill children. And my dad is a part of this? A part of mass murder? What am I going to do?" Her eyes teared up, so I took her hand and squeezed.

Trying to reassure her, I said, "We're going to stop it, that's what. Samantha, you slowed them down by taking the money. I'd like to think that if we just keep you out of sight for the next few days and they can't pay, then what's-her-name will just go home. But there can be no doubt that if she doesn't hand over the virus willingly, they'll find another way to make her, so we can't rely on that to happen."

Kurt said, "Dude, perhaps we should call Homeland Security and let them know about this. I mean, they have to be onto something, right? When I hacked back and came across Fazil's name, they were on my ass within minutes. Let's just tip them off and let them handle it."

Samantha threw up her hands in exasperation. "And tell them what, exactly?" Samantha asked. "That a group of evil Satanists plan on attacking kids with a killer virus? Released by a computer, no less? Come on, Kurt. Say that out loud and listen to how it sounds. And what's our proof? No way. Not a chance. Then there's Vic to think about."

I shoveled more biscuits and gravy into my mouth. "How so?" I asked.

Samantha said, "Look it, if we tell them the whole story and they really do investigate, then how are you going to explain the trail of bodies you've left behind? *I* know they were in self-defense, *you* know they were in self-defense, but will they believe it?"

"Well, I would rather avoid going to jail for the rest of my life. So we take care of this ourselves. I'd rather do that anyways. The Church made this personal when they killed J.B and Ian and then shot me in the chest."

With sudden realization, Kurt asked, "Wait. We're dealing with Satanists? The bad guys are devil worshipers? Jesus Christ."

I said, "We may all want to stop taking the Lord's name in vain, considering we need all the help we can get."

Samantha said, "They'll never let you rest, now that they know who you are. The Church never forgets."

I smiled and said, "Then I'll make sure to give them something to remember." I asked Kurt, "Does this virus chick have a photo we can look at?"

"Sure. One sec'." After a moment of typing, he turned his laptop around. Raakel Korhonen's bio page on the Virasynth website showed an attractive middle-aged woman with long blonde hair and an easy smile. Definitely not your prototypical terrorist. Then again, greed knows no particular look.

Her company bio said she got her Bachelor's at Oxford and her PhD at New York University in bio-genomics. The bio listed a ton of awards and accreditations and she had been working at Virasynth for just over ten years. Sounded like the lady knew her stuff. Which meant if the virus is as deadly as she is good, then there were a lot of children in real danger.

I said, "One person we can call is the Hand of God. Now that there's an actual physical attack on someone, maybe we can get him to jump in."

"Uh, you guys have been leaving out a few things. Just who is this Hand of God person?" asked Kurt.

"Picture someone like me, but working directly for God. On His orders. Kind of God's bounty hunter."

He looked back and forth between us. "You can't really be serious. God's bounty hunter? Satanists? Dude, you're punking me, right?"

When I shook my head "No" he put his head in his hands and I thought for sure he was going to cry, but he pulled himself together and asked, "Is there anything else you've been holding back?"

And I thought what the hell. If he was going to help and risk his life, he should know it all. So I told my story again, this time not leaving anything out. I wasn't sure he could get any paler, but I was wrong. He excused himself and ran to the bathroom.

Samantha said, "Cute guy, but he's not exactly 'hero material'. Are you sure you want him involved in this? I like him. And I owe him for helping to save my life. Things could get really bad for him if they learn who he is."

"That's why I told him the whole truth. But I need him. Look what we've already learned with his help. He'll be O.K. once he stops throwing up."

"Does he do that a lot?"

"Usually only around pretty women. I'm surprised you haven't caused him to have dry heaves."

While Kurt was in the bathroom I got up and went to pay the bill. They joined me at the register and we went outside. I said, "We need to know about that flight. I know a guy with the T.S.A. Let me call him and see what he can tell us."

I found his number and rang him up. Lucky for us, he was at work. I told him what I needed to know and he promised he'd get back to me in just a couple of minutes.

I hung up and the three of us sat on the bench outside the restaurant enjoying a glorious morning. There was a nip in the air, but the sky was pure blue with just a couple of wisps of cloud. It was mornings like this that always renewed my faith in God.

My phone rang and I answered, "That was quick. What'cha got for me?"

Satan replied, "A long and painful death, followed by an eternity of torment. Good morning, Victor."

Chapter Twenty-Two

"Well, if it isn't Luci. Don't count your tortures before they happen there, big guy. You don't have me yet."

"You would be better served by showing more respect. One day soon I will rule in Heaven. And even if I don't, at the rate you're sending people to spend eternity with me, you won't be far behind them. Either way, eventually you'll be mine and I will remember your insolence."

Samantha's eyes went wide when she heard me use the Hand of God's pet name for Lucifer. I angled the phone so she could listen as well. When Kurt looked at us she mouthed the word "Satan" and Kurt about had a conniption, lowering his head to his knees and wrapping his arms around his legs.

"And perhaps I might just be the one to find a way to kick your sorry ass. What do you want, Luci? You're spoiling a great morning that the Lord hath made. Amen, glory hallelujah."

"Where's the girl? We had a deal. You bring her to me and I free your brother's soul."

"It wasn't really a deal. You made me an offer: find the girl in exchange for my brother's soul. You also gave me 'til six P.M. It's not six yet, so you'll just have to wait, won't you?"

"Where is she?" I could tell by the sound of his voice he would definitely have a special place in Hell just for me if he could ever get his hands on my soul.

"Disney World. She's probably on Space Mountain right this very minute."

This got me another roll of the eyes from Samantha.

"Bring her to me now and not only will I free your brother's soul, but I will make you a king among men."

"Tempting as your offer is, I have to decline. Selling his soul to you didn't work out too well for Mikey. I'm afraid you'll just have to wait." My phone beeped and I said, "Hey Luci, I'd love to chat, but I've got a call coming in. I think it's a telemarketer and I'd rather talk to them than you."

"Don't you dare--" I did and hung up on him and answered the other call. It was my friend from the T.S.A. "The private charter is an hour behind schedule and will land around noon. They're coming in at the Louisville Express Charter hangar, right off Grade Lane. You can see the hangar they'll arrive at from the end of the ramp. I'll let you know when they're here, cleared Customs, and what car they pick her up in." He paused. "Vic, is there anything we need to know about this woman?"

"No," I lied. "I hope she's going to lead me to a guy I'm looking for. As far as I know she's just a science geek. But the people she's meeting with, one of them has a guy working for them that is on the run. I follow her, I get my guy."

I thanked him and disconnected the call. Kurt said, "You get phone calls from Satan? I think I'm going to puke."

"Yeah, but it's not like we're B.F.F.s. Or at least I sure as hell hope we're not. O.K. according to my contact, they have a car arranged to meet her at the plane. He'll let us know when they pick her up, what the car looks like, and then we can follow her to her destination and decide what to do next."

Kurt asked, "Speaking of what to do next, have you decided what you're going to do about your brother? Or her? Dude, you only have eight hours to make a decision. Have you decided?"

Samantha and I sat looking at each other, with Bob Evan's customers coming and going. I searched her face for what she might be thinking, but this woman had one hell of a poker face.

I took a deep breath and though I was talking to Kurt, I looked Samantha in the eyes and said, "Yeah. I guess I have. I'll have to find another way to save my brother. Turning Samantha over would mean a lot of people could be hurt, especially if the Church gets their money back. Besides, she's only tried to help things. If I turned her over to Luci, I don't know if I could live with that. I'll just have to think of something else."

Her stoic demeanor broke and I could see relief pass across her features. Samantha asked, "How much do you trust Kurt?" Kurt began to sputter and she leaned over and kissed him on the cheek. He went from sputtering to deadly still.

I said, "You can trust him. He wouldn't be here if you couldn't. Why?"

She said to Kurt, "If I give you my account numbers and passwords, can you hide the money somewhere else?"

Kurt stuttered out a, "Sure." She spent the next few minutes dictating to him account numbers and passwords for accounts at several different banks. He asked, "I'll let you know where I've parked it once it's all moved."

"No. I don't want to know. If they catch me, I can't tell them what I don't know."

He said, "True. That means I'll be the only one who knows. So..." He trailed off and his face took on a green tinge.

I said, "Kurt, they don't know who you are. Samantha only knows your first name. To find you, they'll have to go through me, and they won't be able to do that."

"Look, Vic, you're the baddest dude I know, but everyone has a breaking point...even you."

"Alright. Let's do this. You find places to move the money and when it comes time to enter passwords, I'll do that part, so that they would have to have both of us to get the money. Perhaps I can use the cash as leverage to get my brother loose while keeping Samantha out of it."

"O.K. But man, you have to make sure they don't find out about me. He looked around, suspiciously. "I don't want to do it here, though. We need to go someplace a bit more private."

We went to the nearest library where Kurt and I spent time hiding thirty million dollars. I could tell Kurt was nervous by the way he had to keep backspacing while typing, something he never did. Samantha sat where she couldn't see what we were doing, flipping through a Rolling Stone Magazine.

I had Kurt put just under ten grand into his own account. When we were finished I said, "With only you knowing the account numbers and me the passwords, they're screwed. I think it's time you take a vacation, Kurt. Someplace far from here. If I need your talents for anything else, I can call you and you can do work for me remotely. Your time as a field operative is over. You said you've been wanting to take some time off, so here's your chance. Thanks man, you did great work last night."

"You watch your ass, Vic. There are plenty of people trying to get a piece of it." We said our goodbye's and Kurt even managed to give Samantha a hug without getting sick.

As she watched Kurt drive off she asked, "So. What next?"

"Time to get the Hand of God involved. If killing children isn't going to do it, nothing will. Then we find out where the virus chick is going."

I dialed the number Montoya gave me and he answered on the third ring. I said, "Remember me?"

"Sí, señor," replied the Hand of God. "I trust Miss Tyler is alive and well?"

"She is, and we've got the low-down on what we think the Church is up to. They're going to kill kids and lots of them." I then spent the next few minutes lining out what I knew about Korhonen and what we suspected she and the Church had planned.

"It is God's will you have been brought into this, Victor. Our paths now cross. I am in Louisville looking for a man who holds a high position for the Church of the Light Reclaimed, one who is involved in the Church's attack plans on every level, but who has remained...Como se dice? Elusive. He goes by the name Belial, but I have not been able to find out his real name. He is supposed to be at a meeting here. If she is in town, then perhaps she will be meeting with this man. Do you know where she is going?"

"Not yet, but I will. Her plane lands at noon. Care to join us?"

"Sí. Where can I meet you?"

"There's a gas station right when you get off of the exit for Grade Lane off of I-65. We'll meet you there at 11:30." He agreed and hung up.

Samantha's T-shirt had writing on the front that said 'Unless your name is Google, stop acting like you know everything.' So not only is she drop dead gorgeous, she also has a sense of humor.

She said, "We finally get his help, but only after David is murdered and others are killed. If God has a plan, it sure is one screwed-up plan."

I called Winston and gave him a rundown on what we learned and he agreed to meet us at the station. Finally, we were getting a handle on what Lucifer and the Church planned to do. If we could stop the virus before my six P.M. deadline, I could try and negotiate with the Devil on a soul buy-back plan and free Mikey from Hell.

We got to the station and found Winston waiting in his blue Jeep Grand Cherokee. I pulled up next to him and rolled down my window so we could chat. He looked none the worse for wear following our overnight raid. We made small talk until Montoya walked up to

Samantha's side of the Chevelle and tapped on the window. Where he came from I have no clue, as there was no other car in the parking lot. The dude sure had a habit of just popping up out of nowhere.

Samantha rolled down her window and Montoya leaned in. He said, "If I may make a suggestion. Why doesn't la señorita ride with your friend and you and me ride together."

Samantha looked at me and after I nodded, she shrugged and got out of the car with Montoya taking her place. After Samantha climbed in with Winston, Montoya said, "They'll have to pass by here to get to the interstate. Why don't you have your friend wait a few blocks up? When they leave, we can alternate chase cars, so not to bring suspicion."

His suggestion made great sense. I also got the feeling he was trying to get me alone or perhaps away from Samantha. Either way, as we needed his help, I told Winston to do as he said and we would call him when the Swedish chick was headed his direction.

I could see concern on Samantha's face, but gave her my best smile and she and Winston pulled off. I said, "O.K. Now that you have me alone, what did you want to talk to me about?"

"I learned you let the Church take Miss Tyler away from you. It is good to see you got her back."

"I didn't let them *take* her, they just did. And yes, I got her back. Just how did you know this?"

"I have my own sources inside the Church. They are very upset you kill one of their young Hellhounds."

"Holy crap. Young? You're telling me that thing was a small one?"

"Sí, they can grow to be quite large. You have kill a vampire and a Hellhound. Maravilloso! But you are also killing men at an alarming rate." He shook a finger at me and said, "You must be careful, amigo. You are breaking one of God's commandments and doing so with little regard to how it affects your own soul. In your mind, I am sure the killings are justified and perhaps they have been. Don't cross the line to where you are doing things to save your brother and that lead you on a path away from God's grace."

I could feel myself getting hot under the collar. Here the Hand of God was lecturing *me* about the exact same thing he does and it made me feel like a little kid being dressed down by a disapproving parent. "You don't seem to have a problem with it. How come you get a free pass with killing people? Tell me that, Oh-Wise-One."

"I do not have a problem with it as my soul was lost a long time ago. I kill now, but only those deserved of God's wrath. There was a time that was not the case. I work now to make amends for the terrible things I have done."

I nodded at his gang tattoos. "You were a member of a Mexican drug cartel. You're talking about things you did for them?"

He looked out the front window at the planes taking off and landing from Louisville International. "Sí, señor, I kill my first man at the age of diez, ahh, ten. I work first as mule, delivering drugs. Then a man tried to steal the drugs from me rather than pay the money he owed. I knew what the man I worked for would do to me if I came back without the money. The man who took the drugs laughed at my face and turned to walk away. I pulled out a gun and shot him in the back. Many time I shot this man, to send a message to anyone else who would try and do the same thing."

"I feel nothing following his death. No anger, no sorrow, no remorse, nada. My employer found out. Soon I no longer delivered drugs. I delivered 'messages.' By the time I was sixteen, I'd kill dozens of men, even women. Soon I became the cartel's top assassin. I killed whomever they told me to kill and for a handsome dinero."

Listening to him talk I felt like I was in another place. The words he used, a mixture of Spanish and English, and the cadence, took me back to trips I had made to Mexico. His voice was rich and easy, the kind of voice to make women swoon. Around us people went about their business, with no clue what was going on around them. Montoya told his story without shame. Just told it as if it happened to someone else.

He continued, "Then, one day they had a new 'message' to send to a man who'd stolen money from them. The man had tres chicas bonitas— three lovely daughters, all under the age of twelve. They sent me to kill his children, but to leave the father alive.

"One night when I knew he was gone, I broke into the house and went into the bedroom of the first child. She was ten years old. When I closed the door behind me, there she was, sitting up in bed waiting for me. She said God told her I was coming and that she wanted to pray for me and asked if that would be O.K. I nodded. She closed her eyes and then prayed for me and her sisters. When she finished, she said 'muchas gracias'."

Montoya swallowed hard. "I killed so many, but no one had ever pray for me or accepted fate as this child. For the first time in my life, I couldn't do it. I stood there unable to speak, unable to move. She opened her eyes and looked at me and said, "You have a choice. You don't have to do this anymore." And then I cried, something I had not done since I was a small boy. I cried and could not stop. It took many minutes for me to get control of myself. When I did, I awoke the mother, gathered up the children and then hid them with someone I trusted.

I then went back to the compound of the man that I worked for and killed him and the men with him. Los mate a todos. *All of them.* I spared the women and children of his family, but killed everyone else. I left Mexico. I wandered for many months, and then found my way to Brazil. There I stopped at a small church. I'd never listened to a Catholic Mass, but I did that day. When it was over, I entered the confessional and unburdened my soul to a small town priest. He heard my confession without interruption or condemnation. When I finished, he blessed me and said there was a way out for me, a way to try and make good on the evil I had visited upon the world.

"He put me in touch with a man that would forever change my life. Since then I have been the Hand of God, doing what is asked of me and removing some of the truly evil people and things that are among us. So when I tell you I know how easy it is to lose your soul, I know what I am talking about. I kill as easily as you breathe. I was born with a talent to kill other men and before I was renewed, I did so, with no thought of God."

He paused for a moment, and then continued. "You have been walking a fine line, Victor, and it can be easy to fall on the wrong side. I know you want to save your brother, but I will tell you again: he cannot be saved. He made his choice. If you turn this woman over to Luci, not only will you be sealing your fate, but you will *not* save your brother. I do not even know if my own soul can be saved. I just do, today, what I should have been doing all along: and that is serving God."

I was floored by his story. I could feel my eyes filling with tears forming while he talked. This man had led a life I could barely comprehend. I knew what he was telling me was the truth about my soul, yet I also knew I would still do everything I could to save my brother, short of handing over Samantha. I'd always been able to solve problems and I felt I could solve this one, too. I had always wanted to be the hero.

Now I had to wonder if I would end up losing my soul like Montoya.

My phone rang and my T.S.A. contact told me the plane would land in ten minutes and the plane's guests would be picked up by a white Mercedes limo. I thanked him and hung up. I then called Winston to pass on the info.

Montoya and I sat in silence, each lost in our own thoughts, until the plane, which looked to be some type of Gulfstream, landed. The limo drove out onto the tarmac, the driver got out of the car, and stood waiting by the back passenger door. A few minutes later, the plane's door was dropped. Customs cleared the crew and passengers. Then Raakel Korhonen got out with two other men who followed and seemed demure in her presence. She wore a black pant suit, her blonde hair tied back. She walked as if she owned the world. If the Church paid off, she would certainly own a larger part of the planet. The men were dressed in well-tailored suits and each carried a briefcase.

The driver opened the door for the three of them and they got inside. After closing the door, the driver and one of the pilots transferred luggage from the plane to the car. There were several small suitcases and I wondered if the killer virus was possibly hidden in one of them.

Twenty minutes after arrival, the limo finally pulled out and I called Winston to let him know they were on the move. The limo made the turn to go toward I-65 and I fell in line several cars back. I felt like Ahab following his white whale, but at least the car would be easy to follow.

We passed Winston and Samantha, who were waiting in a McDonald's parking lot and they joined the wagon train. The limo took the ramp to head towards the southern part of Louisville, with us right behind them.

I asked Montoya if he recognized any of the people and he said he didn't. Neither of the two men looked to be Church maniacal leader material. But the guy he was after may have been in the car already.

The limo got off on the Gene Snyder Freeway and headed into a more rural part of the county. Winston and I alternated who would stay with the limo, with one or the other of us passing them and getting off an exit and then switching lead, always keeping several cars between us.

The limo left the interstate and entered an area of multi-acre estates. We had to drop further back as there was very little traffic on the road and we were a quarter of a mile or so back when the limo put on a turn signal and drove down a tree lined driveway.

I pulled over and stopped by a low stone wall that encircled the property. I reached into the back seat for a pair of binoculars and watched as the limo stopped in a circular driveway. The driver hopped out and opened the back door.

Miss Korhonen's exit from the car was not nearly as nice as her entrance. The well-coiffed scientist had been replaced by a terrified woman. The two men, who had acted with such deference when they arrived, were anything but that now. One of the men, built like a well-rounded shrub, hauled her out of the limo by her ponytail, kicking and screaming. The other man, who looked like he belonged on the cover of a Harlequin romance novel, grabbed a hold of both her legs as they carried her to the front door of the house, which was out of my field of vision. The driver got back into the car and started back up the driveway. I gave Montoya a blow by blow account and asked what he suggested we do.

"Have your amigo in the Jeep follow the limo and let us know where it ends up. As they did not remove the luggage, if she has the virus with her, then it will be with the car. Have him call immediately if anyone else gets out of the car. You and I will visit the residents of this house and introduce ourselves."

I drove on past the driveway to the house, calling Winston and telling him to head back the other way and wait for the limo to pass and then to follow it and report where it stopped. I was more than a little pissed we wouldn't have time to pick up Samantha. She would be safer with Winston than she would be with us, at any rate. But not having her with me bothered me. I tried to put her out of my mind for a moment, as for the second time in less than a day I would be storming the castle to rescue a damsel. Or to kill her.

Chapter Twenty-Three

Montoya said, "Pull up to the driveway and park. We'll be polite and knock. If you see either of the men, leave them to me."

"No problem, Kemosabe." He gave me a confused look, but I waved him off.

The house, a two story Williamsburg-style home with blue siding and white trim, was gorgeous. We walked to the front door and Montoya reached under his jacket and pulled out a gun with a short suppressor already attached. I pulled out my Glock and held the gun down by my leg. He looked through the glass panes on either side of the door. Seeing no one, he turned the knob and found the door unlocked, so he opened it.

We stepped into a front foyer opening into a combination sitting room and dining room. Antique furniture gave the room a very warm, inviting look. Yet, once we were both inside with the door shut, the house felt...wrong.

I know no other way to describe it. The house looked Norman Rockwellian, but gave off the vibes of Norman Bates. A grandfather clock located on a far wall made the only sound I could hear, with a steady swish of its pendulum.

A hallway ran off to either side of the front door. Across the room I could see an entrance that revealed part of a kitchen on one side and some kind of TV room on the other. Montoya pointed for me to go right, while he went left. I walked stealthily down the hallway and found a large master bedroom with a walk-in-closet full of women's clothes and shoes. There were pictures on the nightstand of children playing on a swing set.

In the master bathroom hung a beautiful painted mural over the Jacuzzi tub. I walked over and took a closer look. It was an outdoor scene with a young woman sitting under an oak tree watching a boy flying a kite. I was stepping away when I thought I saw the woman sitting under the tree turn and look in my direction, which freaked the holy hell out of me.

I rubbed my eyes and leaned over the tub. She had been staring at the boy, but now she definitely was looking straight at me with the kind of smile that would make a sailor blush. She had deep blue eyes with long chestnut hair that fell loosely around her shoulders and seemed to sway in the wind. I tried to look away but couldn't, my eyes drawn to hers. And then I could hear her whispering to me. I couldn't quite make out the words so I strained harder, concentrating on the meaning of what she was saying. She was telling me we would spend eternity together, over and over. The rest of the world faded away and it was just the two of us. My breathing picked up and my heart started to race. The leaves on the tree in the painting stirred with an imaginary and ominous breeze. Sweat trickled down my face and my knees buckled. I kneeled down beside the tub and laid my gun down on the bathroom floor. Mesmerized, I kept my eyes on the woman in the painting.

The words in my head grew louder, as she told me she would never let me go. My heart was beating so fast I thought it would jump out of my chest. Her grin took on a more ghoulish look as I could feel my body ready to explode into a million pieces, with my body responding in a way it would if there had been ten Victoria Secret supermodels in the room, all vying for my attention.

Then the thought of Samantha broke through the tempest and a shot of anger burst through me. I didn't want this paint-by-numbers witch, but the beautiful woman with the sharp pointy sword. The painted woman's face suddenly changed, showing her own displeasure, as she felt the grip on my mind weaken. I embraced the anger and became royally pissed. Then I bit down hard on my cheek, the pain intense, and was finally able to break eye contact with the sinister painting.

I heard a gasp coming from behind me and dove to the side just as one of the men who brought in Korhonen, the one that looked like the romance novel cover boy, swung a large meat cleaver where my head had just been, striking the tub. He'd removed the suit jacket, rolled up his shirt sleeves and now had on an apron, covered in blood.

I snatched up my gun as I rolled on my back and shot him several times in the stomach, driving him across the bathroom, his own blood mixing with that of what I could only assume was the late Raakel Korhonen, as he fell back onto the porcelain throne. Without looking directly at her, I picked up the cleaver and buried it deeply into the cursed mural, splitting the painted lady in half. I thought it best not to look too closely to see if her expression had changed. Take that, bitch.

I moved on through a connecting hallway to the TV room and could see a straight shot to the kitchen. Montoya was on his knees looking at something on the wall in front of him. The stocky bad guy was standing right behind him holding his own butcher knife. I raised my gun and let off a single shot, taking off the top of his head and sending him down.

I made my way to Montoya, my eyes moving around the house, as the feeling of wrongness had just ramped up another level. Montoya's face was bathed in sweat, just like mine had been, as he fought the pull of a large painting framed on the wall in the kitchen. I shot the damn thing without looking at it until it fell off the wall and Montoya lowered his head to the ground, taking in huge gulps of air. After a moment, he looked at me and then to the dead man behind him.

He said, "Muchas Gracias." I offered him a hand up. He stood still for a moment getting his breathing under control, then went and examined the man lying on the kitchen floor. He had found no wallet or any other ID. "No help here."

I nodded my chin at the dead guy and said, "This makes us even. You saved me at the barn, now I saved your ass here. We're all square."

He said, "This is not a competition. While I thank you for your help, my life belongs to God, not you. Your being here is God's will. This painting, however, is not. I have heard of such things. They are called blood paintings. Blood from victims is mixed with the paint and the paintings are created during dark ceremonies from those who follow Luci. Do not look at anything you see on the walls."

"Too late. I had my own 'come to Da Vinci moment' in the bedroom." I told him what happened and that the other guy was also dead. "So the house is working like a Venus Fly Trap. I'm guessing Korhonen has come to the end of the line, if the blood on their aprons is any indication."

He walked over to a double door just off the kitchen and opened them. There were carpeted steps leading down to what must be the basement. He flicked on the light switch, illuminating the stairs, but they disappeared into a pool of darkness about half-way down. The whispering in my mind cranked back up and I could tell from the way his eyes narrowed, he heard it, too. The words were an invitation to descend the steps, of peaceful sleep and burdens relieved.

I asked, "Do we go down there?" I watched as the darkness swirled around the bottom of the steps, like a shark circling a bloodied swimmer in the ocean.

He shook his head. "No, vamonos. There is no one else here and the woman is dead. I will make sure that those who need to know are aware of this place" Good thing, because down those steps is one place I didn't want to go.

We left the house and walked back into the sunshine. The whispering in my head stopped when we crossed the threshold of the doorway. I took a deep breath and exhaled slowly. This looked like the All-American Home. I remember reading *The Amityville Horror* when I was a kid, a story about a haunted house. I never believed in that kind of stuff, but it was fun reading books about it. Living it, though, was a whole different matter.

We got back into my car and I started the engine. I pulled out my cell and called Winston, but it went directly to voicemail. It didn't even ring. I waited a moment, then dialed again with the same result.

I put the car in drive and headed back the way we'd come. "I got a bad feeling about this. I never should have let her go with him."

Montoya said, "You worry too much. Perhaps they are just in a place where there is no signal. It has happened to me since coming here to your town. He will call when he can."

Was it possible Montoya was right and Winston was just in a no service zone? I thought about it and didn't think so, not with how the last night had gone. The other problem was I also had no way to track Samantha's movements. After she found the Spark Nano in her coat at the motel, she had thrown it into a trash can as we left, and I didn't try and stop her. Now with time ticking down to the six P.M. deadline, I'd lost control of the one thing everyone wanted. What I wanted.

Inside, I was fuming. And as much as I hated to admit it, I was scared. When I first found Samantha at Double D, I gained a measure of control over the situation. I had some maneuvering room, at least until my brother's deadline. Now I was back where I started. Ground Zero.

But there was more to it than simply losing options where my brother was concerned. My feelings for Samantha were stronger than even I believed possible, considering we'd known each other less than a single day. She managed to touch something inside of me, grabbing hold and not letting go. Wild thought after wild thought passed through my brain, as I dreamed all manner of terrible scenarios.

What if Winston had decided to collect on the million dollar bounty offered to J.B.? He claimed to believe it wasn't worth it. And he'd had no problems when we split up for the night. But perhaps the temptation of having her all to himself proved more than he could pass up. If he had, I'd kill him.

Or what if the limo driver made them during the drive back to town and called in backup? The Church would risk nothing to get Samantha and the money back. They would kill Winston without blinking and Samantha wouldn't be long for this world, especially when they found out she no longer had the money.

My thoughts must have been showing on my face. Montoya said, "Breathe deeply, my friend. You've been under a lot of stress. If you grip the steering wheel any tighter, you will break it off and kill us both. Vamonos to the city."

I nodded and was silent as I drove. It was now just past one thirty in the afternoon. I had less than five hours before my brother died and hopped that express elevator going down. I called Winston's cell again with the same results.

We got to the part of Louisville known as Lively Shively, a swath of heavy commercial development along Dixie Highway in south Louisville, and I pulled over and into the parking lot of a McDonald's. I'd been thinking of how to find Samantha and Winston. I took out my phone and dialed Kurt. He answered and I asked, "If I give you Winston's cell phone number, can you find out where he is?"

"Dude, if his phone is on, and if he's in a service area, I can get you close. But not, like, in his pocket. Why? Have you lost him, too?"

I gave him the short version and Kurt said, "Damn, Vic. Not good. Hang tight and I'll get back to you in a bit."

I put the phone on my dash and gripped the wheel tight with both hands. Montoya sat in the passenger seat, with the breeze drifting through his open window, waiting like a coiled spring. I thought about Samantha, how she said she didn't want to die and how with me she felt safe. I could feel the anger boiling over. Anger at possibly losing her. Anger at my brother for selling his soul. Anger at the world in general.

I seethed while waiting for Kurt to call back. When the phone finally rang, I snatched it off the dash and said, "Tell me."

"Dude, they're at a rest area right off I-65, the one just past the exit for Shepherdsville. The signal isn't moving. Get your ass on the way and I'll let you know if he starts moving."

I floored it heading out of McD's and before long I was flying down the interstate and made it to the rest area in a time Dale Earnhardt Jr. would've been proud of. There were only two cars in the front lot. I was about to pull in when Montoya pointed towards the back lot where Winston's Jeep was parked sideways, taking up two parking spots. I pulled up and parked in front of his Jeep and Montoya and I got out.

No one else was parked in the back lot and as I came up to the driver's door, it was clear no one was inside. I could see blood on the seat and opened the door. His cell phone had fallen down onto the floor board.

Montoya approached the passenger side and said, "Victor. Come, look."

I walked to his side of the car and saw on the ground next to Montoya's feet a severed arm. It was dressed in what looked like the sleeve of black coveralls and appeared to have been cut with a very sharp instrument. Samantha had at least been fighting when she was taken. The question now was if she'd been taken alive. Blood soaked the ground, but there was no way to tell if any of it was hers.

The anger that had been building inside me, stopped and hardened. With it came a certainty and calm. They had her and I planned on getting her back, no matter what it took. No matter whom it hurt.

Montoya said, "I am sorry, Victor. We have lost her, perhaps for good, as well as your friend driving her."

"Not yet we haven't. I know someone who might know where they are." I called Kurt and said, "We found Winston's Jeep. They're not here. I think the Church has them again. You said last night that they made a stop at their geek's home. I need his address."

Kurt gave it to me and asked, "What're you going to do?"

"Time to deliver them all to Hell."

Chapter Twenty-Four

Lincoln Townsend's Cherokee Park neighborhood bordered the park itself, with his backyard looking out onto the golf course. The curving street, lined with old oaks and maples, featured a mix of home styles. Townsend lived in a three-story Victorian home, with a well-manicured front lawn and a flower bed surrounding the front. Not the kind of place I would have expected from a geek Satanist.

Montoya and I parked down the street watching the house. We had moved the guns from Winston's Jeep to my trunk, then Montoya drove it and we dropped it off at a nearby shopping mall. We left the severed arm in the rest area parking lot.

We could see a white van parked in the back. Never a good thing with these guys, as vans tended to mean dead bodies. I had to force myself to sit still and analyze the situation. My desire was to drive up, kick the door down and start shooting whoever got in my way. But if Samantha and Winston happened to be inside, rushing in could get them killed. After our last midnight rescue, you could bet your ass they wouldn't be as easy to take down this time. And if he had a pet Hellhound, then things could get even more interesting.

Montoya once again sat silently, observing the scene, seemingly unfazed by the latest developments. I know he had no emotional ties to either Samantha or Winston, but he could show some genuine concern, at least. Inside I was boiling, though on the outside, I was projecting as much calm as the Hand of God. For better or worse, I was at peace with whatever came next. The Church and Lucifer started this war and I was damn sure going to end it. If that meant taking out most of the Church in the process, then I was O.K. with that, despite Montoya's warning about my soul being in danger.

We'd been watching for about twenty minutes, when the van pulled down the driveway and away from us. The only person visible was the driver. Time to make a decision: follow the van, or see whether Townsend was home. Montoya looked at me and I decided the time had come to make a house call.

I reached into the backseat for a small gym bag. I unzipped and took out a hat with the local electric company logo on the front, a clipboard and pen. I used this ruse a lot to gain entry to a home.

I said, "I'll walk to the door and try to get in. The moment you see me make it inside, come on in and join the party."

"Be careful, Victor. And remember what I have said about your soul. You do not want to end up in Hell with your brother."

I just nodded and got out of the car. I walked down the sidewalk in front of the house and paused to look at my clipboard and then at the surrounding houses, just in case anyone was watching me.

I then walked up the driveway, keeping my eyes focused on the clipboard, the brim of my hat hiding my eyes. I made it to the front door without anyone shooting at me, or a Hellhound bounding out to chew my legs off and considered that progress.

I rang the doorbell and started whistling and tapping my pen against the clipboard. After all, no one would ever begin great mayhem while whistling a happy song. I found myself whistling *Sympathy for the Devil* by the Rolling Stones, when the door opened. A man about thirty years old, medium height and wearing Buddy Holly glasses said, "Yes? What can I do for you?"

I squinted at the clipboard and asked, "Are you Mr. Townsend, 1614 Cherokee Trail?"

"Yes. That's me. What's up?" He had a 'no' cares in the world demeanor about him. Much different than Kurt, who seemed like his body had been made for someone else. Lincoln knew who he was and loved it.

I said, "We've been having a problem with the meters out your way and I'm doing a quick check of them in your neighborhood. But I have a couple of questions first, if you don't mind.

"Fire away. Although I have to tell you, my bills have been in line, so I don't think there's any problem with mine."

I took a casual glance around and didn't see anyone else. I pointed to the top page on my clipboard. "Is this your full address and phone number?"

When he bent closer to look at the page, I head butted him hard in his left temple. My mother claimed she used to drop me on my head often, which is why it was so hard. You would have thought I'd found a power switch and turned it off the way he fell to the ground. I stepped into the house and closed the door, pulling my gun. There were steps going up and a hallway leading away from the door towards the back of the house, with a room on either side. A quick glance into both side rooms showed they were empty. I knelt and checked Townsend for a weapon, finding only a cell phone, which I pocketed.

I stood, taking Townsend by the collar of his shirt and dragged him down the hallway. I stopped and listened at the foot of the stairs, but didn't hear anything. I continued down the hallway and made it halfway when a man stepped into it from the backroom. Seeing me, he reached for a gun he had in his waistband, but way too slowly as I shot him several times in the chest. The blood oozing through the shirt told me that he didn't have on a vest.

I heard the front door open behind me, and Montoya stepped in and then closed it again. He took in the situation quickly and held up a hand for me to stop. I did and he moved past me further down the hallway with his own gun out. When he got to the end of the hall, he quickly looked around the corner to his left, and was greeted with gunfire hitting the wood next to his head. He waited a moment and then turned the corner, gun raised, and fired.

I followed him, dropped Townsend for a moment and cleared the kitchen. I glanced into the living room and saw two men Montoya had shot dead. The two men in coveralls had conveniently fallen onto a large piece of plastic spread out to protect Townsend's light-colored carpet from dripping blood. Winston's blood. They had him tied to a chair in the middle of the room. His face showed bruising from where they'd been working him over. One eye was nearly completely swollen shut. And his shoulder was bleeding from what looked like a gunshot wound.

He looked at me with his good eye and said, "Damn, Vic. Your timing is for shit. I had them right where I wanted them. If you'd given me another couple of minutes, I would have kicked their asses."

"Yeah. I can see how you were putting a hurt on them." I holstered my gun, untied him, and then helped him over to a really expensive looking sofa, which he promptly started bleeding all over. The wound on his shoulder was bad, but didn't look life-threatening.

Townsend was starting to come around so I picked him up and tied him into the same chair Winston had occupied. For a second time in less than twenty-four hours, I'd replaced a Church victim with a Church member.

Montoya came back from checking out the rest of the house. "She's not here."

Winston said, "Nah, man. They dropped her off somewhere else, then brought me here. They had me tied up on the floor and I couldn't see where it was exactly. I could see the tops of some warehouses, but not much else."

"I bet he knows," I said pointing at Townsend. "What information were they trying to get out of you?"

"Just what we knew and how we knew it. They have a real hard on about finding you, though. Deveraux wants you bad. I guess you must have messed that pretty boy up but good from what these guys were saying. He plans on doing much worse to you if he catches you."

I looked at Montoya and asked, "You know about Deveraux. I still don't know why you haven't taken him out."

Montoya said, "I want the man above him. Belial. I have been hoping he will lead me to this man. So far he has not. He will face judgment before God soon enough."

I asked Winston, "Can your shoulder handle a few more minutes while I get some information out of this guy?"

"It's all good, man. I'm just kicking back and taking it easy." He said this with a smile, but I could tell he was hurting like hell.

I walked over to Townsend and lifted his chin and said, "Lincoln. Look at me. Do you know who I am, you son of a bitch?"

He did and I could see fear in his eyes. He looked at the dead men on the floor around him, at Winston sitting on his couch bleeding, and the Hand of God leaning against the far wall. He would get no help from those two.

"Yep. Times have changed, Linc'. And if you don't answer my questions fully and honestly, then you'll be joining the others bleeding out on your carpet. Do you understand?"

He nodded yes and I slapped him on the side of the head. "I'm sorry. I couldn't hear you."

He winced with pain and tried to curl up into as much of a ball as the ropes tying him to the chair would allow. "Yes. Please don't hit me."

"Where is she?"

"I don't know. I swear. I don't know."

I pulled my gun out and placed it between his eyes. "Not an answer that's going to help you stay alive, Linc'. Let's try this again. Where is she?"

"I can't tell you. They'll kill me if I do. I can't die. I can't go to..." He stopped and stared at me with pleading eyes.

"Go to Hell? Yeah. I know about how you work for Satan. I've met him. And you're right. He'll be royally pissed when you get there. But that's where you'll be in just a few minutes if you don't answer my questions."

He swallowed hard, took a deep breath and said, "I won't tell you."

"Have it your way." I moved the gun from his forehead and put it against his left knee and pulled the trigger. The sound was deafening in the enclosed space. Lincoln started to scream the moment his knee exploded in a cloud of bone, ligaments, tendons and blood. He pounded his other leg on the floor and rocked the chair as intense pain flooded his brain. At least the plastic was keeping it off his precious carpet.

Montoya came off the wall and took me by the arm and said, "Victor, you cannot do this, my friend. This is torture and it will blacken your soul. You cannot do this to him. If he will not answer you, then so be it."

I shook him off and rounded on him. "I don't give a rat's ass right now. They'll kill her once they find out she no longer has the money. This is my best and maybe only hope of finding her. And don't forget, they plan on killing children. Don't you care about that?"

"Of course I do. You know this. But we will find another way to stop them. Not torture, that's evil."

"Back off, man. I don't want to throw down with you, but I will if I have to. God gives us free will to make our own choices, right? Well, this is MY choice. So back the hell off."

We both had our guns out, both of us holding them casually at our sides, both knowing the other would kill, if needed. I stared into his eyes, watching for any sign he had decided I'd gone too far and needed to be taken out. He seemed to be looking into my eyes just as intently. After a few tense moments, he nodded his head slightly and stepped back, sliding his gun back under his jacket and holding his hands loosely at his sides.

I turned my attention back to Lincoln and, using my gun, pushed his head back so he could look at me. "That's just a taste of what the next few minutes will be like. I don't have time to fuck around with you, so let's cut to the chase, shall we?" I lowered my gun and pressed it against his crotch. "I'm only going to shoot you one more time. I'm going to turn you into a eunuch with my next shot and let you bleed out slowly, tied to this chair. You're going to tell me what I want to know or you're going to Hell in the most painful way I can think of."

"Wait. I'll tell you. Please." He sobbed for a few minutes. "They took her to a warehouse where they're working on the Exodus Project. I have the address in my laptop. It's upstairs in my bedroom."

Montoya said, "I see one on a small desk. I will go get it."

He left and I continued the grilling. "I'm going to ask you other questions, some of which I know the answer to, some I don't. The moment you lie to me, I pull the trigger and we walk out of here." I pressed harder with the gun to make my point. "So you guys plan on releasing a virus during the academic challenge in December, using the aerosol canisters in the computers you're donating, right?"

His eyes widened. "Yes, but how do you know that?"

"Never mind how. How did Korhonen get the viruses into the country? Between Homeland Security, the T.S.A., C.I.A, we have safeguards against that kind of thing. How'd you guys pull it off?"

"The virus was hidden inside the plane itself, inside fake soft drink cans in the plane's refrigerator. We have an inside guy with Customs in the Helsinki Airport and he cleared them to be loaded. When the plane refueled here before the flight back, we had a crew come on and clean the plane, taking the cans off with them. Then they took them to the warehouse, where another group was waiting to transfer the virus to the aerosol cans."

"What type of virus? Anthrax? Bubonic Plague?"

"A genetically engineered version of bird flu. Her company has been testing different combinations to see how easily the virus can make the transition to humans from animals and then a vaccine for it when it does."

Montoya walked back into the room with the laptop. He sat in another chair, placed the computer in his lap, opened it up and powered it on. Lincoln's eyes were starting to get a glassy look as shock set in, so I slapped him across the face, refocusing his attention back on me.

"And I'm guessing they created one that can. They must have found a way around the protein receptor problem."

"Yes. You know about virus transmissibility?"

"I read a lot, so I'm smarter than your average bear. How contagious and what's the projected mortality rate?"

"Highly and over eighty percent mortality rate. When this is released into the schools, the kids and anyone who comes in contact with it will come down with the virus and most of them will die."

"Jesus. Why? How can you be a part of this? Killing kids? Man, that's beyond evil."

Tears streamed down his face. "Because I don't have any choice. I sold my soul when I was a teenager. I agreed to do whatever I was asked to do by the Church. If I don't, I go straight to Hell. The Lord of Light has promised me a high seat when he claims his rightful seat on the throne of Heaven. I do what they ask, and I'm rich here and in the afterlife."

"What you don't seem to realize is just how royally fucked you really are. How does Fazil Al Haqar figure into this? You guys hook up with one of the world's top terrorists to kill babies?"

Townsend actually smiled, and then snickered, despite his pain. "That was my idea."

And then I knew. "He's not involved, is he? You're just going to pin it on him. That's what the labels were for, so that people would blame Muslims. You must've set up the documents for the shell companies that own Inspirational Global Software. You knew the powers that be would track down the whole thing and then pin it on Muslim extremists for the attacks. Satan then has the two major religions at war with each other. It will be total chaos."

Townsend nodded and said, "Muslims and Christians will be killing each other in the name of God. Just like they have been for hundreds of years. Fanatics of each religion will want to kill each other even more and people on the fence about God will tune out and forget about Him all together. A win-win for the Lord of Light."

"Dude, you are so hosed. Satan has lied to you from the start. All you've bought is a one way ticket to Hell. Out of curiosity, why's it called the Exodus Project?"

Townsend was starting to go pale from the blood loss and he'd begun to sweat. But his eyes were on fire. "It's payback for what God and Moses did to the Egyptians. Exodus Chapter 11, verse 5: *And all the firstborn in the land of Egypt shall die, from the firstborn of Pharaoh that sitteth upon his throne, even unto the firstborn of the maidservant that is behind the mill; and all the firstborn of beasts.* God started this fight. We're just bringing payback. The Lord of Light plans to kill as many Christian children as possible."

Montoya said, "His laptop is password protected. What's the password?"

Townsend told him a string of numbers. Montoya entered them and a moment later I heard the Windows sound. Townsend mumbled, "Look in my Outlook Contact folder under Warehouse."

Continuing my interrogation I asked, "Who do you work for? Who's your boss?"

"Preston Deveraux. I take orders from Preston."

"Who's his boss?"

Townsend licked his lips and looked to the side. "I don't know." I pressed the gun painfully into his crotch, making the man squeal. "I swear I don't know. They call him Belial, but I don't know his real name. All I know is he owns the warehouse the operation is going down in. I've never met him and that's all I know."

"And a man with your talents never looked up who the owner is? I find that hard to believe."

He said, "Don't you get it? They find out I've been looking into things like that and I'm as good as dead. When they tell you not to do something, you damn well better not do it. And trying to find out Belial's real name would be suicide. He's one of the most feared individuals on the planet."

Montoya said, "We find the owner of the warehouse and we find out who is the boss pulling the strings for the Church of the Light Reclaimed." He started typing keys and a minute later he said, "The address is 1624 Cane Run Road. Perhaps you can have your amigo find out who owns this building?"

I felt as though my whole world had collapsed in on me. I staggered back a couple of steps until I hit the edge of a coffee table and sat down.

Winston asked, "What the hell's wrong with you, man?"

"I know who owns the warehouse."

Chapter Twenty-Five

I can remember the day Mikey called me to show off his new purchase down at Louisville River Port. The building, brand spanking new and over five hundred thousand square feet, was equipped with every modern convenience. One day he gave me a tour and he sounded like a proud papa of a favorite child when talking about the place, showing me the ultra-modern control room which ran the nearly totally automated warehouse. Put in a code and the product you wanted was brought to the front of the building by automated bots on wheels. They could monitor security from the same room, along with a top of the line fire suppression system.

The building's loading docks, with access to the river, allowed product to be shipped up and down the Ohio River. It's close to major interstates for trucking within the US, Canada and Mexico. UPS's Worldport Facility, their largest automated sorting hub on the planet, is close by allowing domestic and international shipments to be delivered quickly. The place helped to give Mikey a leg up on other people in the same business and it cost him millions of dollars to get it up and running, but it was worth it.

I remembered the address because he said 1624 was the year that Louis XIII of France appointed Cardinal Richelieu the chief minister of the Royal Council and only a dweeb like Mikey would know such a thing.

Montoya said, "It's tu hermano. Your brother is Belial." His hand drifted under his jacket and stayed there as he watched me. "Belial is a name used by one of the four princes of Hell. For your hermano to have earned this name, he must be very high in Luci's eyes and truly diablo, Victor."

"Then this makes no sense. If my brother is Belial, then why would Satan end his life? Wouldn't he want him to stay alive as long as possible? It *can't* be my brother." I put my face right in front of Townsend's and said, "Maybe they forced him to let them use his warehouse, just like they forced you to do the shit you do for them. But there is no way my brother is this Belial-character. How do you know Belial owns the warehouse?"

"A couple of weeks ago, I heard Preston talking to Congressman Tyler on the phone. He told the Congressman that Belial had set up a clean room at his warehouse to handle the transfer of the virus into the individual canisters. Belial owns the warehouse."

"Your brother is one of the baddest Mofos on the planet, and you didn't know?" asked Winston.

"It's not like we pal around together, or anything. He's always been the black sheep of the family. But no, man, I had no clue."

Montoya stood up and tossed the laptop to the ground and once again pulled his gun and pointed it at me. "You must realize now, there is no doubt your hermano cannot be saved. Why Satan has decided to call in his contract now I don't know, nor do I care. I am under orders to find and send Belial to Hell, and I will do so. Please put your pistola down."

I walked over to him, raised his gun hand and put the barrel in the middle of my forehead. "No. I won't. If you're going to shoot me, then do it. I'm going to the warehouse to free Samantha. Then I'm going to find my brother and get to the bottom of this. All you have is this loser's word that my brother is Belial. For all you know, he's making this up just to screw with me. You heard what Winston said. They want me bad. Maybe this is part of their plan, to sic you on my brother and on me."

Townsend nearly choked in panic. "It's not. I swear it. I don't know who you are or who your brother is. All I know is Belial owns the warehouse. Please. I swear I'm not playing games here."

I stared at Montoya a moment longer, and then went back to Townsend. At least the Hand of God didn't shoot me in the back when I turned around. "Have you ever been to the warehouse?"

"Yes. I helped set up the computers there."

"Then you met Michael McCain while you were there?"

"I have no clue who you're talking about. None of the computer guys were named Michael."

I pressed my gun into his groin and said, "I told you if you lied to me I would shoot you and let you die."

He screamed, "I'm not lying! I'm telling the truth!" And I could tell he meant it.

"So you have a security key to get into the building, right?"

"Yes. It's in my wallet. It's white, with a series of numbers along the edge. My wallet is on the kitchen counter."

I went to the kitchen and returned with the key card. Montoya still had his gun out, but at least it wasn't pointed right at me. I went back to Townsend, unbuckled his belt and pulled it out of his pant loops, then wrapped it around his leg and cinched it tight, using it as a tourniquet.

I said, "It's your lucky day. You get to live a while longer." I said to Winston and Montoya, "They have an underground parking garage, but you need a security card to get in and they have a camera recording everyone that passes through the gate. If we just drive up to the door, we've got no chance in hell of getting in. With dipshit here, we can."

Montoya stepped in front of Townsend and asked, "How many men can we expect to find there? Where is this 'clean room'?"

Townsend grimaced, and said, "I have no clue how many men will be there. I wasn't involved in the planning of the actual transfer of the virus. I'm guessing not many. I mean, they think no one knows where and what they're doing. Plus, they didn't want workers there the day they did this. So, the warehouse guys have the day off. They think the building is going through a software upgrade on the systems, so the robots won't work. There won't be many people at the warehouse. The clean room is on the third floor in the back corner."

"Why take Samantha there, but bring Winston here?"

"Belial wanted her there." Townsend pointed at Winston and said, "This guy they didn't care about, but they wanted to learn what he knows. Since you guys knew about the safe house in the country, they decided to interrogate him at my place where we could count on privacy. Or so we thought. But the girl, he wanted her with him."

Montoya said, "That means if your hermano needs Miss Tyler to win freedom from his contract, he now has her and no longer needs your help. He will no doubt turn her over to Satan. If we don't find and free her, she is as good as dead."

I said, "Then let's get moving. We can drop Winston off at University Hospital."

Winston said, "Uh-huh. No way, man. I'm coming with you. I owe these bastards. And you're not leaving me behind."

"Dude, you've been leaking blood for hours. I don't think that's a wise move."

He said, in a very bad British accent, "It's only a flesh wound." He stood, somewhat unsteadily. "Besides, I know the address and if you drop me off at University, I'll just get a cab and show up anyway. So you might as well take me with you."

I offered my hand and he took it. I said, "J.B. made the right choice when he picked you to be his right hand. You're one tough son-of-a-bitch."

Montoya and I helped Townsend out to his car, a brand spanking new Lexus LX SUV. It still had that new car smell and darkly tinted windows. We put Townsend in the back, and Winston kept a gun pressed to his side. We moved all our gear and weapons into the Lexus. Then I got behind the wheel and Montoya in the passenger seat, and we were off.

As I pulled down the driveway and into the street, I asked Winston, "So what happened with the limo?"

"Ambushed, man. The limo driver pulled around back at the rest area and parked. I pulled into a spot in the front, on the far end, and watched. The guy got out of the limo and then walked into the woods. He was gone for like ten minutes, so we figured he wasn't coming back. We drove around to take a look inside the limo. Just as I put my car into park and Samantha opened up her door, these guys come charging out of the woods, guns raised. I didn't even have time to get my gun out before one of them shot me. Lucky for me, it just grazed my chest, but it bled like hell. So I played up being hurt, hoping they would let their guard down and I could make a move, but no such luck.

You should have seen your girl. They went to grab her and she had that sword out of its box and took one guy's arm off and stabbed two more before they tased her and took her down. That's one woman who I'm going to stay on her good side. That's one fierce lady. They threw us in the back of the limo, dropped her off, then brought me here."

I said, "She's something else, that's for sure." I looked at Townsend in the rear view mirror and asked, "Will your key card get us into the control room?"

Through gritted teeth he replied, "Yes. I have master access to the entire building. My card will get you into any part of the building you want." After a moment, he said, "Listen, guys, let's work out a deal here. I know things about the Church of the Light Reclaimed that you guys can use. Get me to a hospital and I'll tell you anything you want. Work with me here."

Montoya said, "I don't think you comprende the gravity of your situation. You are not going to a hospital. And you will tell us what you know as it is the only thing keeping you alive. When we are finished at the warehouse and I have killed Belial, then we shall see what I will do with you."

Montoya kept talking about killing my brother and I didn't know whether I'd be able to do anything to stop him, short of putting a bullet into the head of the Hand of God. I refused to believe my brother could be Belial. Mikey could be many things, but I didn't think killer would be one of them. Especially not killing kids. I just couldn't find a way to reconcile the man Montoya knew with my brother.

But what if Montoya and Townsend were right? My brain pounded trying to manage it all, and I had to push the thoughts away. First things first. Find and save Samantha. Then deal with my brother.

We arrived at Louisville River Port and I pulled in and parked behind a warehouse down the docks from my brother's place. I turned in my seat and said to Townsend, "Here's what we're going to do. We're going to put you behind the wheel to drive the rest of the way. The three of us will be here in the back. If you do anything to alert them, I'll blow a hole big enough to put my fist through. Once we get into the parking garage, we will leave you in the car. Do what we tell you and you get to keep breathing. If not, then it's cancel Christmas for you. You got it?"

He nodded yes and we helped him hobble to the front driver's seat, with Montoya and I squeezing in the back seat with Winston. I got a bullet proof vest out of the back and handed it to Winston, who gingerly stripped off his shirt, put on the vest and then put his shirt back on. I asked Montoya if he wanted one, but he declined.

I asked, "Is that because you're protected by God?"

He gave me a smile more suited to a barracuda and replied, "No, because any man that gets close enough to take a shot at me will already be dead."

O.K. then. I glanced out my window, the heavy tint turning the late fall sunshine into a twilight gloom. With any luck, the tinted glass would keep anyone from seeing us as we entered the garage. I rubbed the barrel of my gun along the side of Townsend's cheek and said, "I don't need much excuse to kill you, Lincoln. Not much at all. And the Hand of God here needs even less. Winston would kill you just for fun. So don't try to be a hero. Just do what we tell you."

With a whimper Townsend put the Lexus in drive and pulled around to the entrance of my brother's warehouse. His face was covered in sweat and he kept licking his lips. I said, "Try and relax Lincoln. Take a few deep breaths and let's get this over with." I handed him his key card.

The building, three stories tall, with loading docks and lifts that allow access to all three levels, backed up to the Ohio River. The wind had picked up and made whitecaps on the river, pushing against its never-ending flow to the Mississippi River and eventually the Gulf of Mexico. The building itself used steel framing and a rough hewn rock exterior.

Townsend pulled up to the card reader at the ramp leading to the underground parking garage for employees, slipped in his security card and the machine spat it back, with the metal grate raising to let us enter. He pulled his car down the ramp and we could see there was only a handful of cars parked in the garage, one of which was my brother's Lexus convertible. I had Townsend back in next to his car and turn the engine off, which he did with difficulty, considering the pain in his knee.

Winston opened up his door and got out, with Montoya sliding out after him, guns out and watching for trouble as I grabbed Townsend by the collar of his shirt and drug him roughly into the back seat while he offered up groans of pain. Using a couple of plastic wrist cuffs I secured him to the child car seat rings, then used some duct tape from my duffel bag, ripped off a piece and covered his mouth.

I said, "If I see you out of this car before we come back for you, I'll shoot you. No second chances with me, Lincoln. Nod if you understand."

He did so and I got out and went to the back of the Lexus and loaded up. I slung the straps of an MP5 over my shoulder, picked up the carry bag with the grenades, extra gun clips, a can of black spray paint and a few other goodies. I handed out com links and each of us slipped them onto our left ear and did a mic test. As ready as we'd ever be, I said, "This is going to take crackerjack timing, Wang."

Winston laughed and Montoya, who obviously had never seen *Big Trouble in Little China*, asked, "Who are you calling Wang?"

"Never mind. Just remember, it's all in the reflexes. Come on, let's get this done." And with that I walked into battle with Winston and the Hand of God.

Chapter Twenty-Six

We made it to the elevators with no problem. I looked around and found a brick by a large dumpster. I pushed the elevator button, but instead of taking them, I let the door open then set the brick by the door, keeping it open and we took the stairs. I didn't want to end up like Jack and Wang in *Big Trouble*, trapped in an elevator and sent to the Hell of the upside down sinners, or wherever the hell they were sent to die was. I took point, followed by the Hand of God with Winston bringing up the rear, and we entered the stairwell.

Just before we reached the first level, I said, "The control room is on the second floor. They may already know we're coming." As I pointed to the security camera in the upper corner of the stairwell, I blew the camera a kiss, took out the can of spray paint and coated the lens.

"As far as I remember, the cameras are video only, no audio. At least they won't be able to see what we prepare. You guys heard Townsend, the clean room is on the third floor, in the rear. We need to get to and take the control room before we head that direction. Once we do, Winston you'll set up there and be our eyes and the cavalry, should the shit really hit the fan."

Montoya asked, "There are executive offices in this building, no?"

"Yes. They're on the second floor, down a hallway from the elevators and across from the control room." Any idiot would know why he asked me that question: the most likely place for my brother to be would be in his office. His office included a large reception area, a conference room with video conferencing equipment and a spacious main office with a sixty inch flat screen TV. My brother had it all and it could end up being his tomb.

We headed up to the next level, so far with no resistance. "Just do me a favor, will you? Before you put a bullet in my brother's brain, let me at least talk to him. You wouldn't be here if it wasn't for my help. You owe me that much."

Montoya considered this and said, "I will do what I can. But if I have no choice, I will not hesitate." And I knew that was as much as a consideration as I was likely to get out of the former cartel hitman. I used the spray paint to cover the second floor stairwell camera.

I said, "I'll open the door a crack and see what's what. Winston, get a concussion grenade ready. If we need to use it, I'll get the door open, you toss and we hit the door hot. Then shoot anything that moves. Any questions?" Neither man said anything.

I took a deep calming breath. I could feel the adrenalin kick in, my heart begin to race, and all my senses become hyper alert. I was now fully prepared for whatever was to come next.

When I first arrived in Iraq, our unit spent time going from district to district clearing out some of the buildings where people still loyal to the old Saddam regime were holed up. It felt just like this. Knowing you were going to kick the door in and might find someone on the other side that wanted you dead—just as much as you wanted to kill them. It made me feel more alive than anything else in the world that I'd ever experienced.

From an earlier visit, I knew the stairwell and bank of elevators opened in the middle of the floor, with a good sized waiting area with a hallway running off to the right that lead to Mikey's office and the control room. To the left, there was a hallway to more conference rooms and the johns. Straight ahead, double glass doors opened up onto the warehouse floor.

The stairwell landing was large enough to allow the three of us to stand to the side of the door that opened towards us. I turned the handle, and pulled the door open a crack, only to be greeted with a hail of gunfire.

I let the door fall shut and thanked God my brother used steel frames and stone walls for this building. The solid metal door pounded with a staccato sound as bullets pounded the other side. I made sure Winston was ready with the concussion grenade. When both men nodded they were ready, I once again turned the handle and this time threw the door wide open.

Winston popped the clip and tossed the MK3 concussion grenade into the waiting room. Designed to be used in enemy bunkers to cause a maximum amount of damage, the grenade roared with the added sound of exploding glass. We hit the room hard, me diving to the left, Winston to the right. The door closed and my brain registered that Montoya had not come through the door behind us. Son of a bitch.

The grenade had done its job, with four men lying on the ground, two of them dead, the other two badly wounded. The glass walls of the reception area had been blown to pieces and dust filled the air. I pointed for Winston to head down towards the control room. I went to the wounded men and took their weapons, while keeping an eye on the warehouse floor, as I scanned for more attackers. I had a clear view down the center aisle to the far end of the building. There were four neat rows of shelving, nearly thirty feet high, packed with all types of products. I knew this floor to be packed with electronics headed overseas, as my brother's clients were mostly international companies.

I could see Winston glance into Mikey's office and evidently he didn't see anyone as he crossed the hall and put his back against the wall, then looked into the control room. He straightened up and held up two fingers: two people in the control room. I pressed my com button and, speaking softly, described my brother and asked him to nod his head if he saw him. He indicated No. I pressed the com button once again and asked for the Hand of God to respond. He didn't. I backed up to the stairwell door and opened it for a quick look up and down the stairs. No Montoya. The Hand of God had decided to do something on his own.

I jogged down the hallway and joined Winston. I told him to watch the hallway while I cleared the executive office. I did so quickly and found it empty. I did find a cup of Starbucks coffee, a venti caramel macchiato, still warm. I made fun of him for drinking these flavored metro-sexual type coffees instead of the real thing. So Mikey WAS here, and just a short time ago. I had to find him before Montoya did, or his ass was grass.

I went back to the hallway and glanced into the control room. A man and a woman, both in security guard uniforms, were hiding behind a counter lined with monitors and computer screens where the warehouse manager could move any piece of product in the warehouse by typing in the coordinates of where the items were stored and entering in a dock location. The robots would retrieve and deliver the stuff and never complain about the workload or the overtime.

I approached the door with my gun raised, Winston covered my rear. I used Townsend's keycard, and the lock lights went from red to green. I opened the door and said, "Stand up where I can see you. Do it now with your hands up and slowly, please."

They did so and I got a good look at both. The guy's eyes kept twitching, while sweat stained the armpits of his white shirt. I've seen cats on a hot tin roof that were not as nervous than this guy. The woman looked at him and said, "For Christ's sake, Ron, grow a pair, will you?" She looked at us and said, "The cops are on their way. You guys will be in deep shit if you don't leave now."

I remembered her from when Mikey gave me the grand tour. It took a moment, but I remembered her name. "Good try, Gloria. I know Mikey wouldn't let you call the cops with what he has going on here today. You didn't call anyone. Now back up."

She squinted at me and then said, "You're Mr. McCain's brother. What the hell do you think you're doing? He's your own brother for Christ's sake. I mean, you come in here blowing things up and killing people. What the hell is wrong with you?"

"You may find this hard to believe, but I'm trying to save his life. And you guys started shooting first. We just took exception. Now where is he?"

Her eyes shifted to the bank of security monitors and then back to me and she said, "I don't have a clue."

"Next time we play poker, Gloria, I hope you join us. But, have it your way." Winston and I used more plastic cuffs to secure the two guards, sitting them on the floor where we could see them. Winston took a seat behind the control panel and took a moment learning how to move from camera to camera as we searched the building for Mikey, the Hand of God, and anyone else.

I asked the woman, "Where's the view of the clean room? I don't see it coming up on the camera rotation."

She shook her head and said, "Because there ain't one. They never did put one in there. The boss don't want no camera in that room. Said there's no need for one there."

I walked over and squatted in front of Ron and used the gun sight on the end of my gun to lift his head by his nose. "Ron, how do we view the clean room? If you tell me there isn't a way, then I'm going to turn your head into something you'd only see in a Picasso painting, capisce?"

Without hesitation, he said, "You can't get to it by going through the rotation. You have to select camera view at the bottom and then type in 69. We're not supposed to look at that room. That's for Mr. McCain only."

Gloria said, "You're such a piece of shit, Ron. You know that?"

"Fuck you. You want to die for these bastards, then go ahead. They ain't paying me enough to go down for them." Gloria just shook her head and then scooted a few feet away from him until I told her to stop.

Winston pulled up the box and entered in 69 and a view of the clean room appeared, if a limited one. We could only see about half the room, which included the door. There were two long tables with all sorts of medical equipment on them. On a section of a counter were dozens of soft drink cans with the tops cut off. On the counter opposite I could see a large quantity of small metallic canisters, which were the ones that would presumably be installed into the computers.

I could see two people moving in and out of the view of the camera. They were in what I always thought of as medical space suits, with full body coverage. Over the span of the several minutes I watched, they moved into view carrying a couple of new canisters then walked back out of view. Mikey must have set the camera up so that you could see who came and went, but not the work being done. At the door, there were two men in coveralls with machine guns cradled in their arms. Whether to protect the people moving the virus or to make sure they didn't leave, I had no idea.

With only Winston to help me, this just became a hell of a lot harder. It was no picnic with only three guys. But the Hand of God is worth a dozen other guys in a fight like this one. And now he'd gone rogue on me. I took a moment to think. My brother had to be here somewhere in the building. If he wasn't in his office, then the next likely place would be the clean room keeping tabs on what they were doing. But if he was there, then he was in the part I couldn't see.

I still couldn't believe my brother was Belial. Mikey lived with a chip on his shoulder, always looking for any sign someone was making fun of him because of his size and always ready to strike out when he thought they were. When we were kids, he had a reputation as a guy you couldn't trust further than you could throw him. But not someone capable of killing hundreds, if not thousands, of people. Could my brother really be capable of mass murder?

I didn't think so, but I admitted to myself I was now having serious second thoughts. There could be little doubt the Exodus Project was going down in his warehouse and nothing happened in this building that Mikey didn't know about. Everything pointed to Mikey being Belial, I just couldn't believe it. Or wouldn't. Winston said, "O.K. I've figured out the cameras. I can keep a view on you as you head up to the clean room. Are you sure you don't want me to go with you?"

"I think we have a better chance with you keeping an eye on things. You let me know what's ahead of me and what may be coming up behind me. It's better than being blind."

And just as I said that, the camera showing the third floor hallway outside the elevators went static, as someone took out the camera. My money was on Montoya and that he was now on the third floor after my brother. "I'd better get moving. If I go down, call the cops and get the hell out of here. You got it?"

"Got it. Be safe, man. Good luck with your brother. I hope it ain't true, you know, this Belial stuff."

"You and me both. It goes without saying, you see either Montoya or Mikey, shout it out." I shouldered the weapons bag and went out the door. Time to go hunting.

Chapter Twenty-Seven

I hit the stairwell and jogged up the steps to the third floor, took a deep breath and opened the door. There were also four rows of shelving on this floor, but with a more wide open floor plan. There were no fancy office suites up on this level, just large warehouse space. I had a clear view down the center aisle where several of the robot forklifts were parked.

The clean room was in the upper left hand corner so I stepped out and moved that direction. I hadn't taken more than two steps when Winston warned me to take cover, just as someone took a shot at me from the far end. I dove behind the closest rack and risked a look around the corner. I could see the man, his gun held at the ready, watching for me. The moment he saw me, he took yet another shot, hitting a box on the rack above my head.

Hitting any target from nearly a hundred yards away is tough. A moving one even more so. I ducked back down behind my rack and considered my options. The shelving here rose twenty feet. I slung my gun around my back and grabbed the middle support beam and began to climb. I made it to the top and eased my way between boxes of cell phone batteries and smart phone cases.

There was a small gap all the way down the racks, and I moved quietly down the length of the aisle. Winston said in my ear, "I have a different camera angle up on your level. There's a bogey with an automatic in the center aisle, headed towards the elevator. I saw you come out of the stairs, but lost you."

I clicked the com once to let him know I heard. I came to a spot where I could see between a crate of gardening tools and a box of lawn furniture. The Church dweeb had almost reached my spot, moving slowly, gun up in the ready position, scanning for me, but not looking up. When he reached me, I grabbed the edge of the lawn furniture box, which said it weighed one-hundred and fifty pounds, and toppled it over the side. He glanced up at the noise and the box hit him smack dab in the face and took him to the ground, where his legs spasmed a couple times and then stopped.

Winston said, "Damn, Vic that looked like the Roadrunner dropping an anvil on Wile E. Coyote." He then started humming *Another One Bites the Dust* by Queen as I slowly walked the rest of the way down the aisle from the top of the rack.

Winston said, "I can see the rest of the floor. At the end of the main aisle, take a left and there's a door. It has to be the clean room. I don't see anyone else."

I'd almost made it to the end of my row when I caught movement from the corner of my eye on the rack two over from me, along the left hand wall. I ducked down and l glanced around the corner of a row of blue plastic containers filled with kerosene. Kerosene is still heavily used in places like Africa for everything from lamp oil to cooking stoves and Mikey made a killing shipping the stuff all over the continent.

I watched for several more minutes, letting my breathing and heart rates slow, and extending my senses. I had no doubt there was somebody else up here besides me. The only real question was: who. Montoya? My brother? Another Church goon? After several more minutes passed, I decided I couldn't wait any longer. I clambered over the side and made my way quickly down the racks and onto the floor.

I pressed my back against the racks and looked up, seeing nothing but kerosene. I moved over to the far wall, trying to find movement, but still saw nothing. I pressed my com link and said, "There's someone else in the racks. See if you can find them. I'm going for the clean room."

"Roger that."

I moved to the clean room door and inserted and then removed the keycard. But the security light remained red. I tried again with the same results. I asked Winston to ask the guards if they could override the security from the control room. After a moment he told me, "Negatory, good buddy."

I found an intercom button next to the card reader and pushed it. After a moment a man's voice said, "There's no way in here. If you don't put down your weapon and step away from the door, we will call the authorities."

A camera was mounted right over the door. I looked into it and pushed the button and said, "I'm here to speak to Michael McCain, not some flunky. Put him on."

"I'm sorry sir, but there is no one here by that name. This is your last chance to leave before we call the cops."

"Look, tell Mikey his brother is outside the door and to get his ass out here."

I waited a few more moments and started to push the button again when a shot rang out and a man dropped from the corner of the far rack, with a bullet hole in the top of his head. I pressed my com button and said, "Winston, far rack, up top.

"I don't see him, man. The camera on that angle is out. Has to be Montoya." I agreed with him and was just happy he wasn't shooting at me.

I looked at the tall stacks of kerosene and my mind flashed back to the barn going up at the farm and decided, fuck'em. I pressed my com and said, "Let me know if the guards inside the clean room make a move to come out. I'm going to turn the heat up on them."

I shouldered my gun and went to the stacks of kerosene, dragged several of the five gallon containers over to the clean room door and emptied them on the wall and the floor. I knew the guys inside would be watching me so I smiled at the camera while I poured. I did this several more times when I heard Winston in my ear tell me the guards were preparing to open the door. I shifted my gun to the ready position and waited, temporarily in a Mexican standoff. I pressed the intercom button and said, "I'll give you guys one more chance to put down your guns and come out. I know you've been watching me and I just poured enough kerosene out here to burn down half of Louisville. So it's now or never." I pulled my lighter out of my pocket. "You try and rush me and all of you die. You stay in there and you die. Lay down your weapons and come out and you at least get to live. You can't win. Give it up."

Winston said, "I don't know what you just said to those dudes. But the scientists inside are freaking out and waving their arms. The guys with the guns just pointed them at the scientists and they have their hands frozen in the air. This is better than watching Law and Order, man."

There was a brief pause and Winston said, "Hey, you said your brother is a little dude, right? Does he have black hair and a Vandyke beard?"

"Yeah, why? Do you see him?"

"I do. He, Samantha and some pretty boy with a banged up face are walking through the second floor warehouse, headed towards the elevators. Mike and the other guy are packing those machine pistols. What do you want me to do?"

"On the left side of the console, you'll see buttons that control their alarm and fire suppression systems. Turn them off then get over there and see if you can slow them down. Cut the leg ties on the two guards so they can get out. I'll be right there."

I wished I could give the people in the clean room more time. But I'd given them their chance and they didn't take it. I thought about the two men who burned to death at the farm. I thought about how Satan had nailed me to a wall and melted my body down to the bone. I searched for something deep inside me that said I gave a shit. I didn't find it.

I stepped back away from the pool of liquid, ripped off the corner of a box on the closest shelf, took out my lighter and set the end of it on fire. The door to the clean room started to open as I tossed the burning paper onto the floor.

The kerosene went up with a whoosh and in a blink the area was engulfed in flames and screams started from the clean room. It wouldn't be long before the rest of the kerosene went up, taking the clean room and warehouse with it. There were times when I wondered if my whole life would turn out to be about fire and damnation, I just never figured it would be, literally, about fire and damnation.

I ran for the door as the room behind me exploded and the other containers of kerosene blew up. I don't know how many people were in the room turning computers into death machines, but they were all about to pay the ultimate price and I could not have cared less. The Exodus Project was now toast, so at least something good would come from the death and mayhem.

I hit the door to the stairs running and could hear gunfire on the floor below me. I took the steps two at a time and hit my com button to let Winston know I was coming through the door.

Winston was at the corner of the waiting area, his machine gun raised, ready to fire. He said, "They split up when I fired a warning shot. Your brother went left, Samantha and the other dude right."

I shouted, "Mikey. It's Vic. I'm coming out to the floor. Don't shoot my ass."

I moved past the four now dead guards, past the broken glass and to the warehouse floor just in time to see Mikey running back my direction. "Vic! Help me! He's going to kill me!"

Mikey threw down his gun and ran towards me. Dominic Montoya, the Hand of God, turned the corner of a row of shelving, and was closing fast on Mikey. I managed to put myself between Mikey and Montoya. "Dominic," I pleaded. "I asked you to let me talk to my brother. Don't shoot."

"I'm sorry, my friend. There is nothing to talk about. There should be no doubt in your mind he is Belial and the man behind the Exodus project, among other diablos you know nothing about. His life is forfeit. Please. Step aside. I do not wish to kill you, but I will if you do not remove."

Mikey said, "I don't know who this nut job is, but I've never heard of this Belial person. Come on, Vic. You KNOW me. We have the girl. I can get my soul back. I swear to God, Vic, I'm a changed man. I'll become a monk. I'll do whatever you ask. Just don't let him kill me. I'm your brother, for Christ's sake. This guy's a liar. You can take him, Vic. You're better than he is."

Winston took a step out and trained his gun on Montoya. "You want me to take him out, Vic? He can't get both of us."

"No. No one's going to shoot anybody. The killing has to stop here."

Mikey dropped to his knees behind me, his arms going around my waist, his eyes wide in terror, as Montoya continued to advance and Mikey could see an eternity in Hell coming his way. I wanted to believe him, but I knew deep in my soul he was lying. But it didn't matter. I couldn't let my brother be shot like a rabid dog.

"Dominic, you have my word. I'll turn him over to the cops. I'll take him there myself. He'll be dealt with. Come on man, you don't have to do this. The Bible is about redemption. Don't do this. I'm begging you. He can change."

I might as well have been pleading with the statue of David for all the good it did me. Montoya said, "I am sorry, Victor. If you will not move, then you shall join your hermano in Hell. Adios, Victor."

A shot rang out.

But, it did not strike me or Mikey. The Hand of God was thrown back as he was shot by Deveraux high in the chest. Winston whirled, ready to shoot Deveraux, but the man had Samantha in front of him, his arm around her neck. Her eyes drooped and her mouth hung slightly open, a small trickle of blood flowing from her temple where he must have struck her. Winston moved back and took cover at the corner of the entrance.

Montoya lay on the ground, his arms and legs moving slowly as he died. As soon as Mikey saw him hit the ground, he stood up and slapped me on the back, and said with a wide smirk, "Thanks, Vic. I couldn't have done it without you."

I turned on him. "You little prick. What've you done? That's the Hand of God. You can't kill him."

"Au contraire, little brother. I believe I just did. Nice shot, Deveraux." He walked over to where Montoya lay and kicked him in the ribs. I felt my brain explode and I took one large step, picked my brother up and threw him against the wall and grabbed him by the throat.

"So help me God I'll beat you to death with my own hands."

Half- choking, Mikey said, "Deveraux, if my brother does not let me go in the next five seconds, shoot the bitch in the head and then him, if you please."

"With pleasure, Belial." Deveraux put the barrel of his 9 in Samantha's ear and started to count out loud.

Winston said to Deveraux, "You pull that trigger and you're a dead man."

Deveraux just continued counting and on the count of four, I let Mikey go and stepped back, my chest heaving. I asked, "So you *are* Belial. Why? Why are you doing this? Killing kids? My God, Mikey, your soul. Don't you know what you're doing to your soul?"

"Your God, not mine. I've made my choice. A war's coming and I want to be on the winning team. The Lord of Light picked ME to be one of the Kings of Earth when he reclaims his place in Heaven."

I felt confused. "But, you said you wanted your soul back, that you would be a changed man. You said you wanted to save your soul. That's why you wanted Samantha, so you could get your soul back."

"I wanted her back because I wanted the money back. You can't run an operation like mine without a good cash flow, Vic. Now that I have her, I'll get my money and be back in business."

Smoke started pouring from the vents high up on the wall, a billowing black smoke. I said, "I hate to break it to you, brother, but your Exodus Project is going up in smoke as we speak. Thanks for putting a rack of kerosene right next to the clean room."

I could see anger flash across his face, but then a smile returned. "Oh well. You know me. I always have a plan B. And a C and a D. You've only set me back, not shut me down."

"Satan says you'll be dead by tomorrow. You won't get a chance to do anything else. You're a dead man walking," I said.

He shook his head and said, "That's so yesterday. I've signed a new contract, Vic. I just had to deliver the death of the Hand of God. And thanks to you, I just did. I'm now first among the four kings of Hell. And I couldn't have done it without you."

He walked up to me and all sense of brotherly love vanished. "I have let you live today because of the love I bear our mother. But if you come after me or the girl, I'll have Deveraux shoot you on sight. Do you understand me?"

"Perfectly. But there's one little problem. She doesn't have the money anymore. I do."

Mikey's eyes narrowed, and then he looked up at the smoke pouring out of the vents. "Maybe you're bluffing, maybe you're not. But I don't have time to sort it out right now. I'll find out from her if you're telling the truth."

I said, "So help me God, if you hurt her—"

"Oh, please. How much has God helped you, Vic? How much does he help any of us? Was God ever there for me growing up? How many of my prayers did God answer? None, that's how many. Not a one. The Lord of Light has given me all I asked for and more."

He walked over to Deveraux and Samantha, stroking her face. "Lucky for her, the Lord of Light has uses for her father. So if she, or you, gives us what we want, she'll live. But we'll be going now. Hug mom for me the next time you see her, won't you? Now step over there, please," he said motioning to the far side of the warehouse, "So I can be sure you won't try something stupid."

I nodded to Winston and we both moved to the far wall as Mikey, Samantha and Deveraux headed toward the steps. After they were gone, we ran to Montoya as the warehouse continued to fill with smoke and breathing became harder.

I bent down to check his wound, but it was clear he didn't have a chance, as blood soaked his shirt. His eyes opened as I knelt over him. Tears filled my eyes and I said, "I'm so, so sorry. I didn't mean for any of this to happen. Please forgive me.

He smiled weakly and said, "There is no need to ask forgiveness from me. You were trying to save your hermano. Only ask for God's forgiveness." He swallowed and said, "Your soul may be lost to you, my friend. There is still a chance you can save it. Go to the Derby Mission on Preston. Ask for Brother Joshua. Tell him what happened." He grabbed my coat and pulled me close. "Tell him I'm sorry. Tell him..." And with those final words, the Hand of God died.

Chapter Twenty-Eight

Winston shook my shoulder and said, "Man, we've got to get out of here. Let's go." I nodded, stood and we both took off for the stairs, and raced to the parking garage. We got to Townsend's Lexus and jumped in. I looked into the back seat, where Townsend lay, his throat slit from ear to ear. Mikey's car was gone and Townsend must have seen them coming and gotten their attention. Too bad for him. I had Winston drag his body out and onto the garage floor.

I threw the Lexus into drive and tore out of the garage. I could hear the sirens approaching the building and took off in the other direction, weaving our way behind other warehouses. In the rear view mirror I could see the whole building was engulfed in flames. The Exodus Project was now up in smoke. We drove slowly out the far side of Louisville Riverport and could see an army of fire engines and police cars now surrounding the building.

Winston whistled low and said, "Man, would you look at that? Your brother just took a huge beating."

I shook my head. "Knowing him, he'll make a fortune on the insurance." We quickly put the inferno behind us and for several miles neither of us said a thing. Then Winston said, "Do you really have the money?"

"Yeah, I was telling the truth. She doesn't have it anymore." I told him how she'd passed the money to Kurt and me. "My brother knows if he hurts her, he won't get a dime from me. My only hope is that as soon as they find out, they contact me to make a deal and I can trade the money for her."

"Are you sure that's a wise move? These are some evil Mofos. You give them the money back and no telling what they have planned next."

"I don't give a rat's ass. I just want to get her away from them and the money is the only bargaining chip I have."

We didn't say anything else until we made it back to Townsend's house to pick up my car. We transferred all the gear and then wiped down the Lexus and the house, and took off. I drove him to the shopping mall to retrieve his Jeep. I pulled up behind it and put the car in park. I offered him my hand and he took it.

"When they call you, you're going to need someone to watch your back. Call me and I'm there," he said.

"Count on it. Thanks Winston. If there is ever anything you need, all you have to do is ask." He nodded, got into his Jeep, fired it up and drove away.

I did the same and headed back into town. In less than twenty-four hours, my whole life had come crashing down around me. The world as I'd known it had been a lie. I went from a raging agnostic to sure that not only did Satan exist, but so did God. I went from having a brother who was merely a pain in the ass to one who very well may be the most evil man on the planet. And I'd gone from a man who had no desire to settle down, to a man who had fallen in love with the woman of his dreams, only to lose her.

I pulled up to the curb near the Derby Mission, a converted former elementary school, that served three meals a day to the homeless in the area and provided temporary housing to many of them as well. It was nearing the dinner hour and several men and a few women hung around outside, smoking and talking, in the late afternoon sunshine.

I got out, locked the Chevelle, and went inside. The cafeteria was already hopping, with the aroma of soup and warm bread filling the air. I asked a man standing in line where I might find Brother Joshua and he pointed to an elderly black man handing out soup bowls at the far end of the line.

He was of average height, with sprinkles of white around the edges of his short cropped dark hair. His arms looked muscular under his blue button down shirt. As I approached, I noticed his eyes. As he spoke to each man, his eyes bathed them with empathy and compassion and the men and women responded in kind. Each person he spoke to continued on to their table with a smile on their face, despite their circumstances. I found myself smiling as well, despite the crap I'd been through over the last twenty-four hours. That was, until he looked at me.

His gaze hit me like a hammer, the compassion gone, replaced by a searing intensity that stripped me down to my soul and found it lacking. He said something to a volunteer nearby and nodded for me to follow him to a back room. I did so, but with trepidation. I knew I was about to be judged and I was, for the first time since I'd been a very young child, afraid.

The room, a small office, sparse on furniture or decoration, seemed to close in on me as he sat behind a battered desk. There was a chair opposite the desk, but I remained standing. He watched me for a moment, then stated, in a bass voice I would have expected on a much larger man, "Dominic Montoya is dead."

"Yes. He was shot and killed an hour or so ago."

"You're Victor McCain?" His eyes continued to bore into me as I told him I was.

"Tell me what happened. Start from the beginning."

And so I did. Starting with the visit from Lucifer through to the death of the Hand of God and the escape of my brother with Samantha. I told him of the men and at least one woman I'd killed. I told him how it was my fault Montoya had been shot. I had confessed my sins many times to our parish priest and afterwards I'd always felt better, as my burdens were lifted and I could go back out and sin again in good faith. But this time, as I finished, tears were streaming down my face and I knew my sins had not been lifted, but instead fell upon me like the proverbial ton of bricks.

I asked, in a quiet voice, "My soul. Is my soul lost?" I trembled standing there, as I knew the answer, but wanted to hear it from this man.

"You have allowed an evil to continue to work its will on mankind and you did so knowing your brother to be Belial. Your pride has handed the forces of Satan a great victory today."

"But I stopped the Exodus Project. Surely that counts for something?" I hated the pleading tone in my voice. I was Victor McCain, bounty hunter. I hunted the most dangerous men humanity could throw at me. I always believed in myself. Now I doubted. Now I was afraid.

"Once the project came to light, it was as good as dead. You could have stopped them in any one of a number of ways. Simply calling the police would have ended any chance they had of success. No. It does not count for something. You had choices and you made them. And where your soul is concerned, you made the wrong ones."

I bowed my head and wept. I knew deep inside he was right. I had killed over and over in the past day and had felt not the least bit of remorse for what I'd done. Shouldn't I have at least felt something?

"There is, however, a way out for you." I slowly looked up and into eyes that seemed far older than the man sitting in front of me.

I said, "Become the new Hand of God. You're going to offer me the same deal you offered Montoya."

He nodded. "I am. The Hand of God spoke of you to me. He said if something should happen to him that you might be a good choice to replace him."

"I have a question." I hesitated for a moment, then asked, "Did he do enough, when Montoya died, did he go to Heaven?"

"I don't know the answer to that question. It isn't for me to absolve him. He now has faced the ultimate justice. His prior life was filled with evil. He had a large slate to wipe clean. For most people who live and die, asking forgiveness is enough. For a handful of others, it is not. I pray he has found peace."

"Samantha said she believed God is dead. I *know* this can't be true, but after the last twenty-four hours, I'm not as sure. How do you convince people with the type of evil that is loose in the world that He's not?"

"I don't know the answer to that question. But then again, it's not my job to have all the answers. My role is to help people live with the questions."

"And if I accept and become the new Hand of God, can I save my soul?"

"I can quote you hundreds of different Bible verses that could come close to explaining your situation, but the truth is, your situation is unique. I do know you cannot if you don't. But understand, once you accept, there is no going back. This isn't a job you retire from. This is a job you die from. You will not die an old man while sleeping in your bed during your golden years. Your death will come sooner, rather than later, and you will most likely die violently. It's your choice. But if you choose to serve as the Hand of God, once you start down that path, there is no other."

I laughed without humor and said, "Like I have a choice."

"There is always a choice. Now you must make yours. Will you be the next Hand of God?"

I took a long cleansing breath and said, "Yes. I just hope I can do justice to the man I'm replacing." Shaking my head, "So what now? How does this work? You tell me what I'm doing, is that it? So, you're what, like Nick Fury?"

"I don't rock an eye patch and you're not Captain America. But yes, I give you your assignments. No freelancing. You don't go after anyone unless I clear it first. You're not a vigilante. You will be doing God's will. From this moment forward, you belong to God and it will be He that passes judgment on you, and may God protect you."

"Fair enough. O.K. then, what's my first job?"

"To complete the job Dominic Montoya was sent to do: find and kill your brother."

A chill settled deep inside me. And I had one thought: this job was going to be a real downer.

The End

Acknowledgments

Many people had a hand in making this novel a reality. I would like to thank Bob Fulks, without whom this book would never have been written. I would like to thank those who read early drafts and let me know where I didn't have a clue: Wendell Farrar, Donna Krieg Monroe, Brad Stiles, Bob Dalton and Tom McNeil. Thanks to Alberto Iglesias for helping to make Dominic Montoya authentic. Thanks to Carol Tway for her never-ending support.

Thanks to the Bluegrass Writers Edge for bringing sanity out of chaos. Thanks to Starbucks Store # 2464 in Prospect, Kentucky who became like family over a cup of coffee. O.K. *several* cups of coffee.

Thanks to my wife Karin who wields the red pen of death before anything I write sees the light of day. Major thanks to my editor Martha Swanson, who treated my work with the right balance of insight, inspiration and insistence. Thanks to Frank Hall and all the great folks at Hydra Publications. Your support and enthusiasm for my work is the best thing a writer could ask for. I would also like to thank cover artist Karri Klawiter for doing a fantastic job turning ideas into reality.

And lastly, thanks to my writing mentor Dewey Hensley for seeing the writer I *could be* and pushing me to be the writer I *should be.*

About the Author

Tony Acree was born in La Grange, Kentucky in January 1963. His short story fiction has appeared in *Kentucky Monthly Magazine*. He has written articles about his time as a stay at home dad for a women's magazine as well as sports and information articles. His work has also appeared in *The Cumberland*, the Kentucky state wide newspaper outlet of the Sierra Club. He is a member of the Green River Writers as well as The Bluegrass Writers Edge, a creative writers group in Goshen, Kentucky, where he lives with his wife and twin daughters. Visit his website at Tonyacree.com. You can find him on Twitter and Facebook. You can email him at Tonyacree@Gmail.com.

Made in the USA
Lexington, KY
27 March 2017